LEARN AND HA

ACTIVITY & GAME BOOK

Basic skills for 6-7 year olds

Teora

LEARN AND HAVE FUN: ACTIVITY&GAME BOOK.
Basic skills for 6-7 year olds

2 Wisconsin Circle, Suite 870
Chevy Chase, MD 20815
USA
for the English version
Translated by Adriana Bădescu

Otto de Mentockplein 19
1853 Strombeek-Bever – Belgium

077

ISBN 1-59496-005-4
Printed in Romania

10 9 8 7 6 5 4 3 2 1

In each row, draw the precise number of objects needed to equal the number indicated in the left column.

6		+
7		+
5		+
9		+
4		+
8	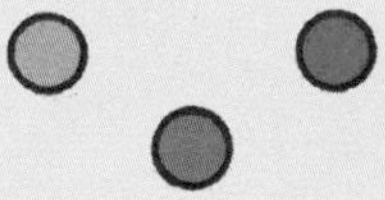	+
2		+
10	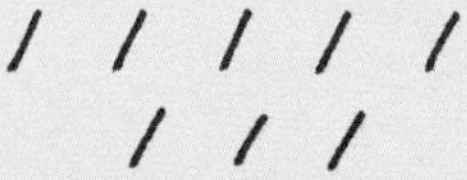	+
3		+
9		+

Connect each picture to its corresponding season.

SUMMER

WINTER

SPRING

AUTUMN

In the following boxes, cross out all of the letters that can be found in the words "ball," "letter," and "chaw."

Try to arrange the remaining letters to make a new word. What word will it be?

l	e	a	b	c	a	t	t	e	b
c	b	o	a	t	b	e	t	l	e
a	t	b	e	c	c	h	l	h	a
b	r	e	e	l	a	t	e	c	h
l	a	t	b	t	a	g	e	b	e
b	l	e	t	t	b	e	t	l	b
a	l	t	a	e	b	b	t	c	e
l	e	f	e	b	t	w	c	b	l
e	b	c	h	e	t	a	r	a	e
b	e	t	l	a	h	b	e	h	c

The remaining letters: ....

The word: ....

1. Connect each animal's name to its baby name.
2. Connect each product to the animal from which it comes.

1.

foal

calf

hen

piglet

sheep

horse

chicken

lamb

cow

pig

2.

wool

caterpillar

milk

ivory

bee

honey

cow

elephant

silk

sheep

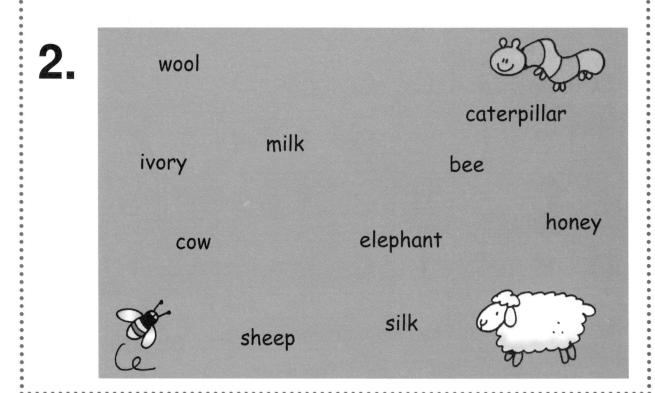

In each row, add all the elements.
Then subtract the ones that are crossed.

	5 - 2 = ...
	... - ... = ...
	... - ... = ...
	... - ... = ...
	... - ... = ...
	... - ... = ...
	... - ... = ...
	... - ... = ...
	... - ... = ...
	... - ... = ...

1. Circle the letters that can be found in the word written in the left column.
2. Connect the letters L R S T to the words that begin with these letters.

1.

bat	r	b	g	y	a	c	f	p	t
pot	g	b	o	e	h	t	m	c	p
star	t	e	a	o	p	r	i	c	s
pigeon	p	i	e	g	u	e	b	o	n
table	t	v	a	b	n	d	l	r	e
tribe	t	b	y	r	u	e	i	y	t
bird	c	i	o	f	r	v	d	b	e
lake	e	p	l	o	u	a	b	t	k

2.

task lake star table road love

shoe light

L R S T

seed row

six tall lock red skate train

Write the missing numbers in the little hearts.

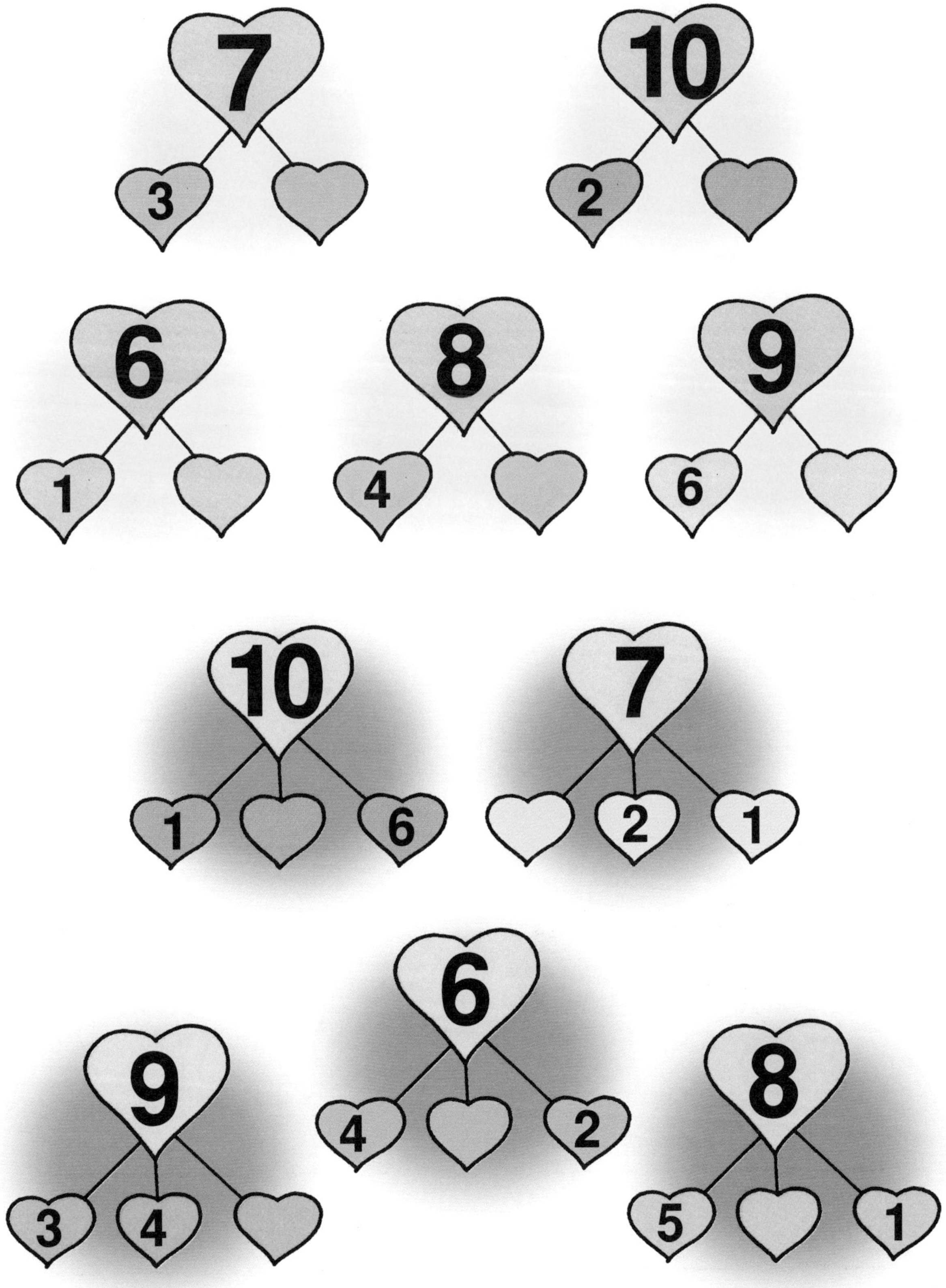
7
3
10
2
6
1
8
4
9
6
10
1
6
7
2
1
6
4
2
9
3
4
8
5
1

Find out what number is hiding in each drawing.
Write this number many times between
the two black lines.

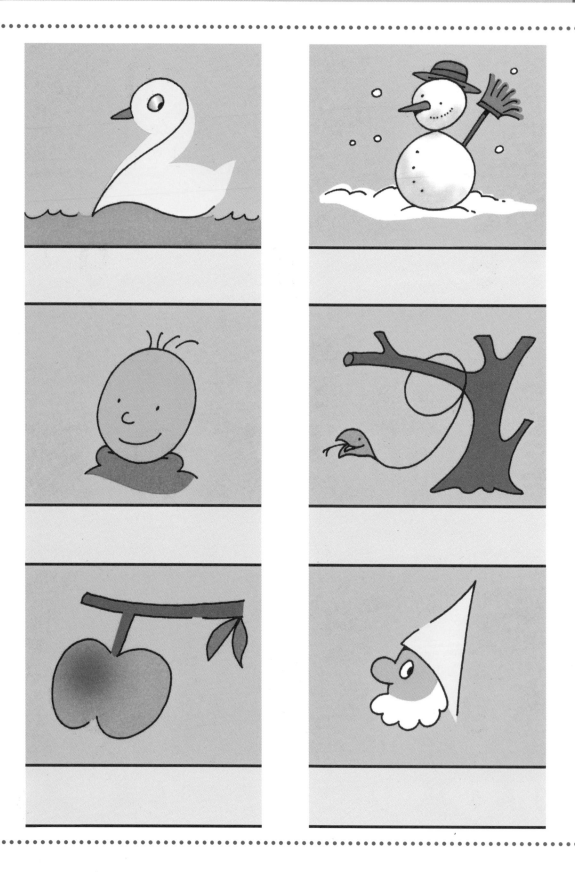

Read the following text aloud.

Hello, I'm Jack.
I live in a house.
The house is big.
The cat is looking through the window.
It is my window.
The cat's name is Fluffy.
Fluffy loves fish.
There is a tree near the house.
The tree is old.
There is a pigeon in the tree.

Do the following sentences tell the same story as the text above? Circle the apple if the answer is yes and cross the apple out if the answer is no.

- There is a tree.
- The pigeon is old.
- I am Paul.
- The house is small.
- Fluffy is the cat.
- The cat loves meat.
- The cat is in the tree.
- Jack lives in the house.

Eric would like to get to his friend. To do it, he must follow a road made of words. Every word differs from the preceding one by only one letter. Help him find the right way across the boxes.

soil

cold	coil	car	square	star
ball	bar	coal	call	barn
tart	coat	tear	part	pear
tower	boat	goat	board	moan
port	start	contour	goal	goose
bear	born	core	store	foal
door	sorrow	fork	fowl	cord

bowl

What is the name of animal that corresponds to each picture? Pay attention, the letters are jumbled!

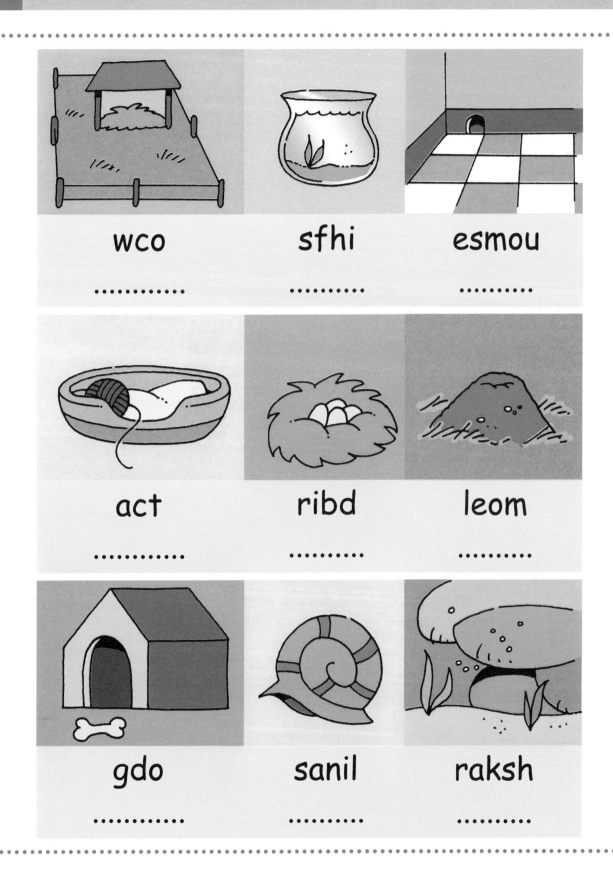

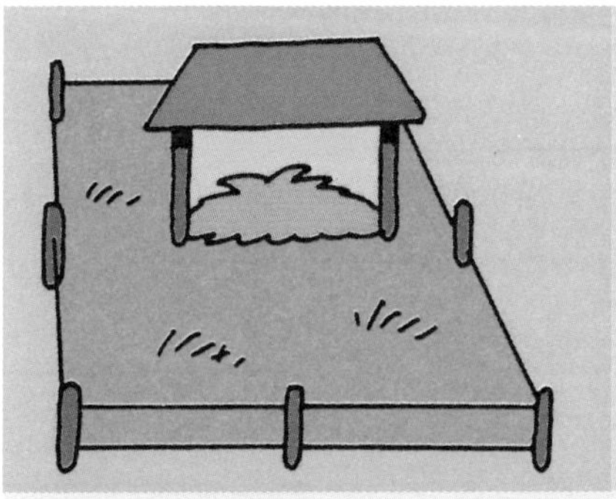

wco

....

sfhi

....

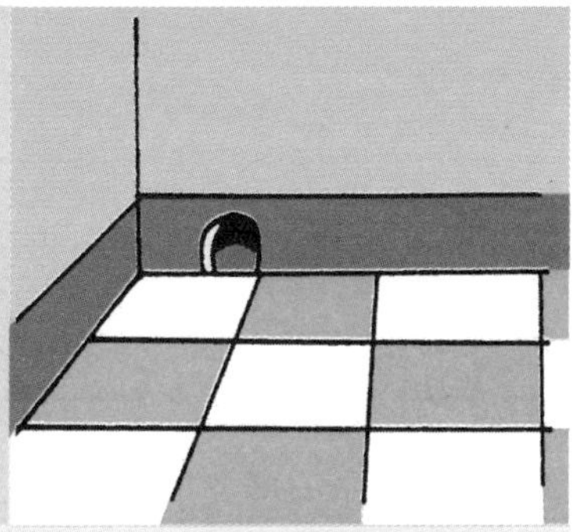

esmou

....

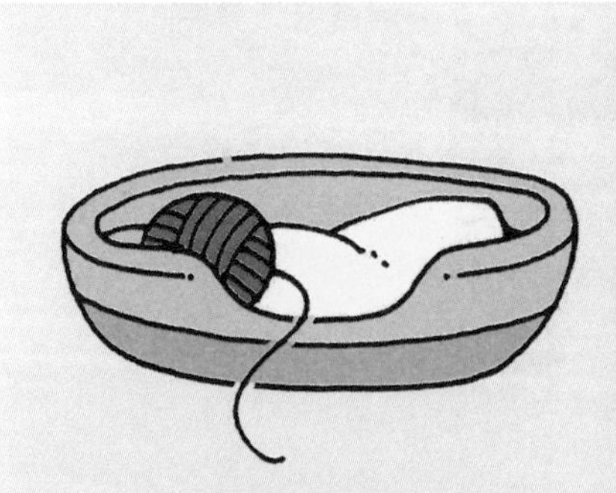

act

....

ribd

....

leom

....

gdo

....

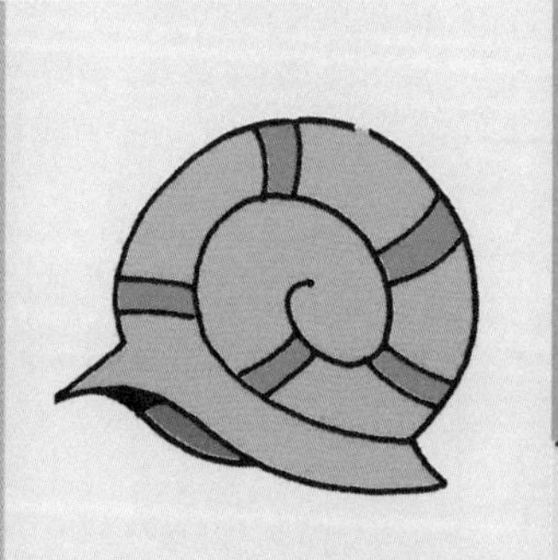

sanil

....

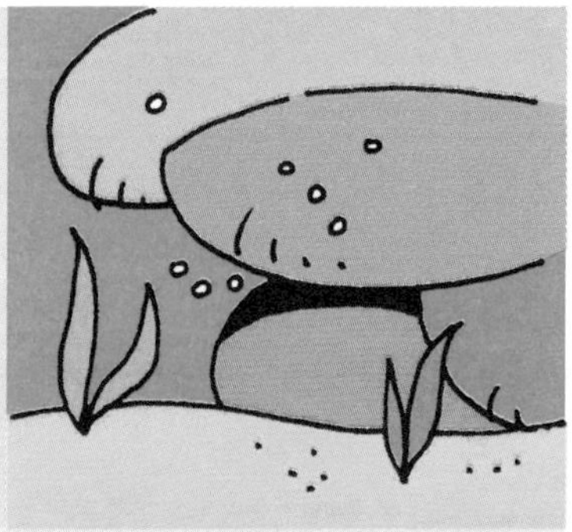

raksh

....

Fill in the dotted lines with the right numbers, so that each row adds up to the number that is written on the top of each box.

	10	
4	2	......
1	......	1
6	......	1
2	7	......
0	8	......

	9	
......	8	0
......	2	4
......	3	4
......	6	1
2	7	......

	8	
1	4	......
0	6	......
2	1	......
......	2	5
3	......	2

	7	
0	2	......
......	1	4
......	0	6
1	5	......
......	3	1

Write the missing numbers in each line.

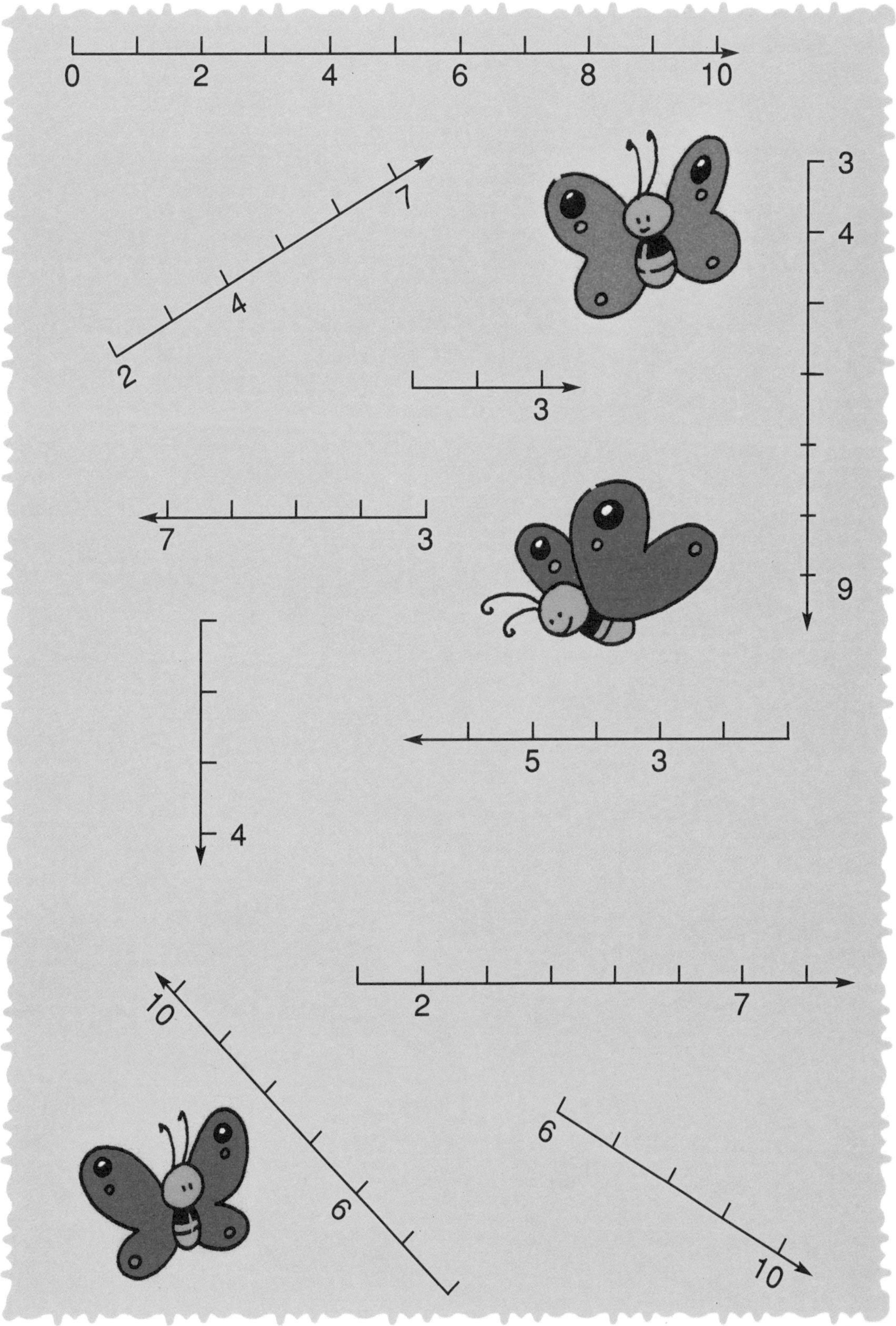
0 2 4 6 8 10
2 4 7
3 4 9
3
7 3
5 3
4
2 7
10 6
6 10

1. Draw the hand that is missing on each clock.
2. Draw the missing hands.

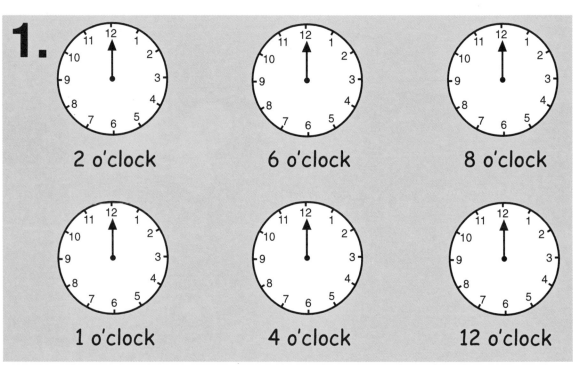

1.

2 o'clock

6 o'clock

8 o'clock

1 o'clock

4 o'clock

12 o'clock

2.

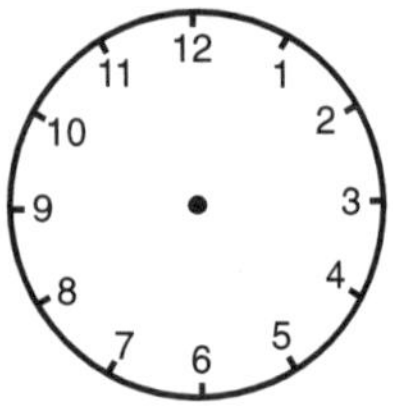

7 o'clock

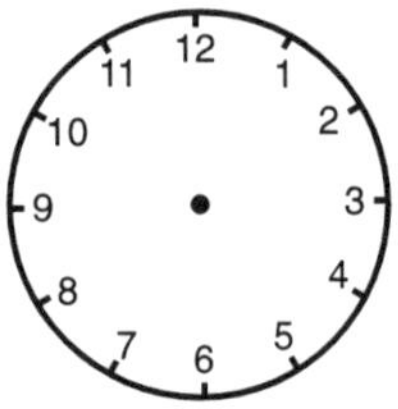

10 o'clock

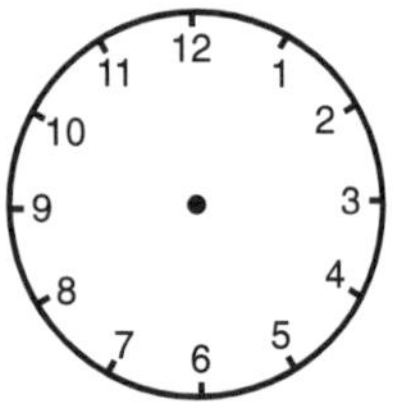

1 o'clock

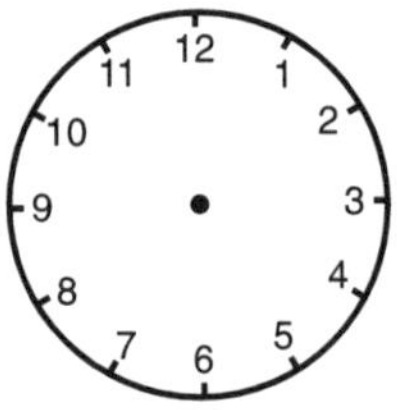

5 o'clock

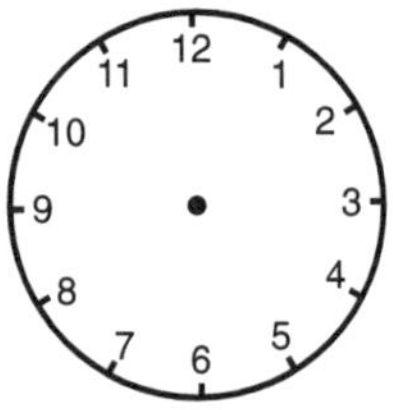

9 o'clock

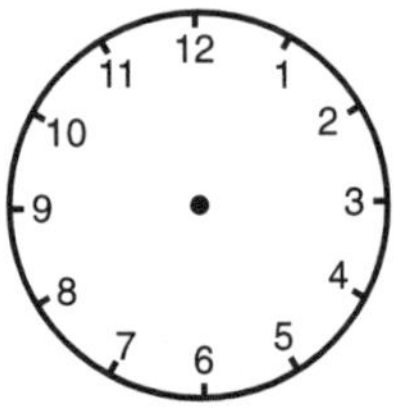

3 o'clock

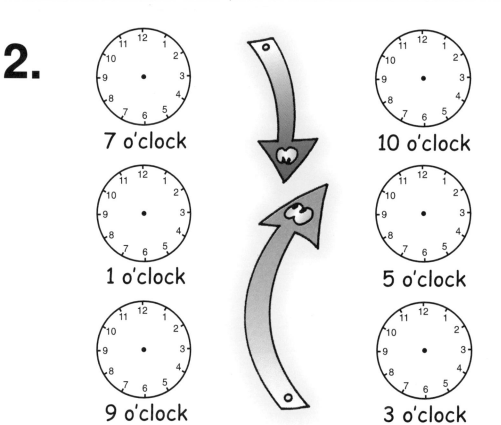

Circle the sentence that matches the picture.

- The cat eats the fish.
- The cat does not eat the fish.

- Ann is eating a pumpkin.
- Ann is eating a pear.

- Jack is under the boat.
- Jack is on the boat.

- Mother wears a hat.
- Father wears a hat.

- Susie is ill.
- Susie is not ill.

- The flower is in the bowl.
- The flower is in the pot.

- The monkey is on the branch.
- The mouse is on the branch.

- The skirt is wet.
- The sock is wet.

Read carefully the following sentences and try to place the action. Write next to each sentence the symbol that corresponds to the action.

Past:  Present:  Future: 

- Tomorrow I will go to the cinema.
- Yesterday I read a good book.
- I am really tired.
- After a week I'll be going on holiday.
- When I was younger, I bothered my sister.
- Later I'll be a musician.
- I am busy drawing a beautiful landscape.
- Julius Cesar was a Roman emperor.
- At four o'clock I'll be at my friend's birthday party.
- Attention, the street light is red.

Add the missing number to add up to the number written in the star.

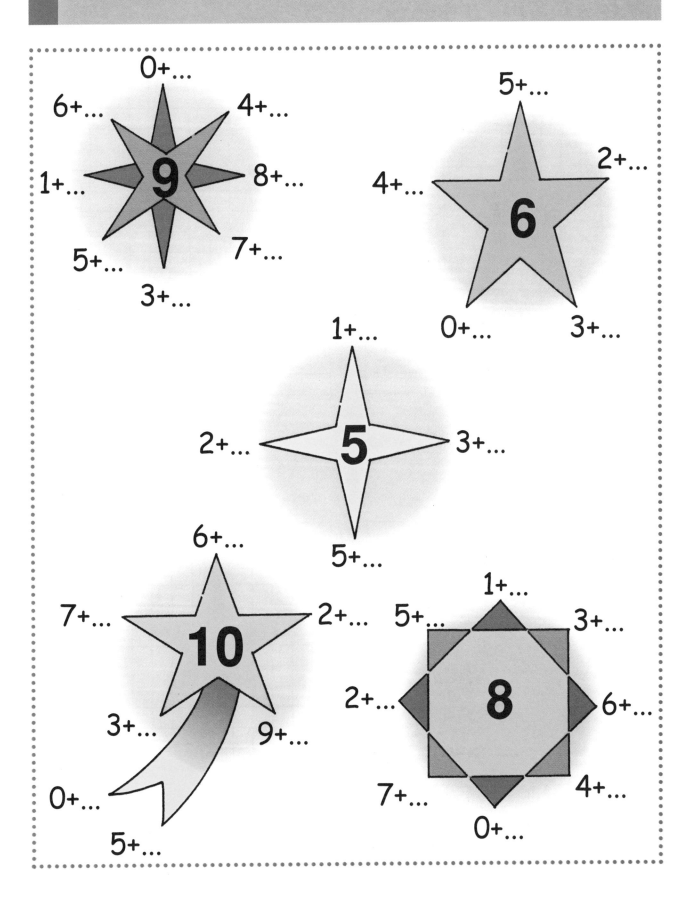

0+...
6+...
4+...
1+...
9
8+...
5+...
7+...
3+...

5+...
2+...
4+...
6
0+...
3+...

1+...
2+...
5
3+...
5+...

6+...
7+...
2+...
10
3+...
9+...
0+...
5+...

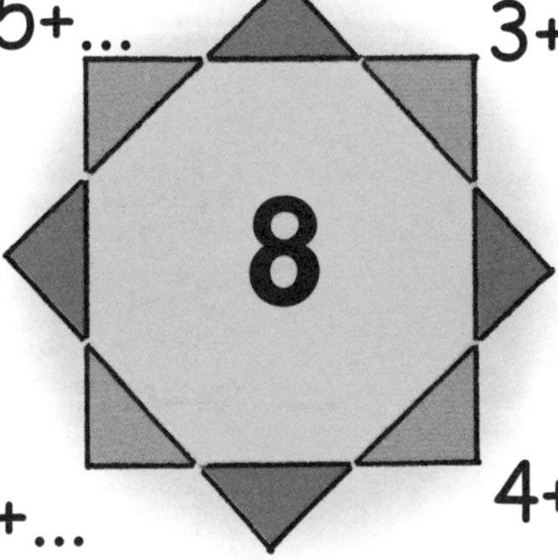
1+...
5+...
3+...
2+...
8
6+...
7+...
4+...
0+...

Try to copy the picture on the left by using a ruler and counting the squares.

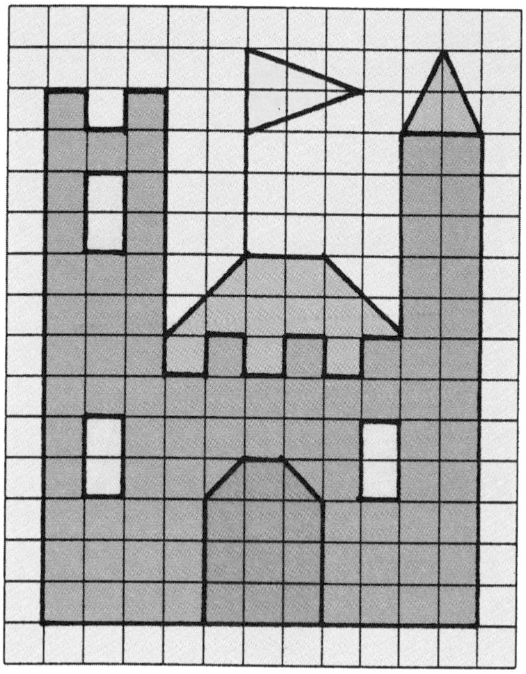

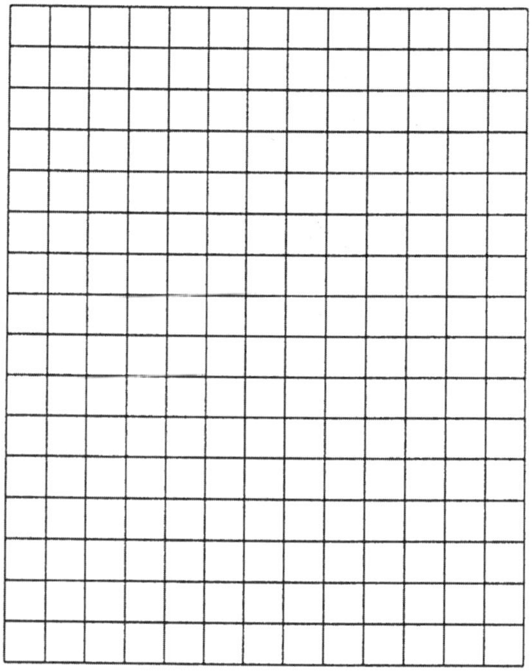

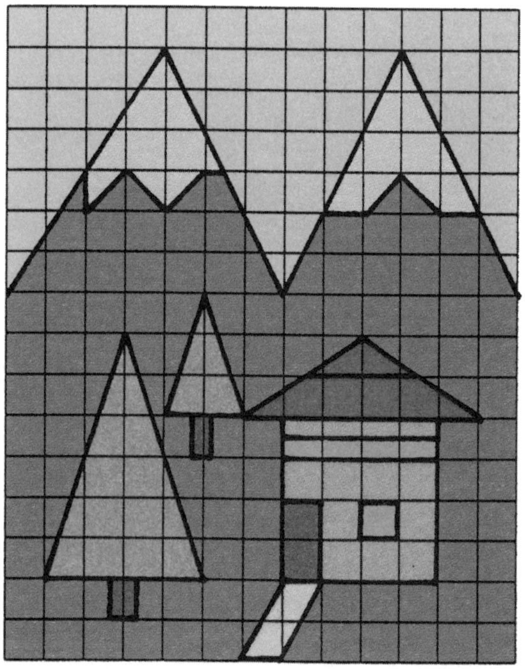

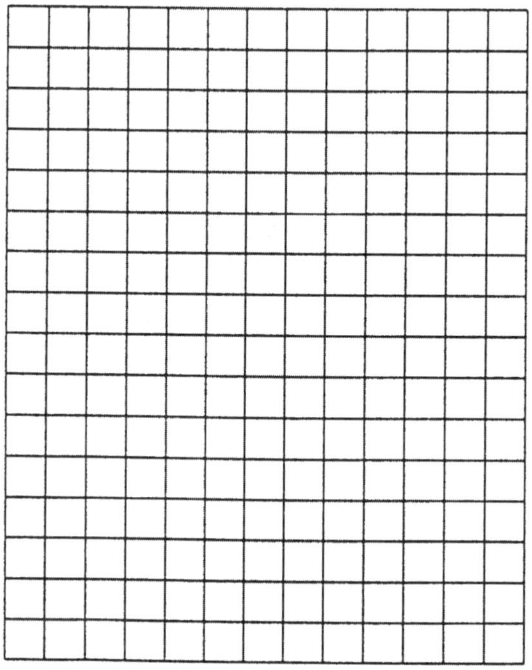

Read the following sentences carefully and you will discover the name of each animal. Write each name under the corresponding picture.

....

....

1. Fluffy is in its basket.
2. Cheeta is eating a coconut.
3. Spike is next to its cage.
4. Ann is giving a ball to Flipper.
5. Tim is eating leaves.
6. Billy is on the rose.
7. Kaa encircles the branch.
8. Sophia laid an egg.

Find the pair of ducks whose sum is 18.
Every time you use a number, cross it out.

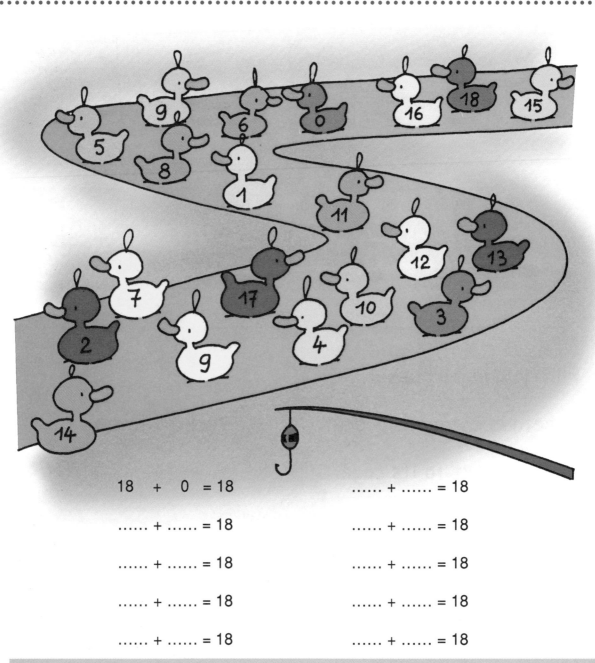

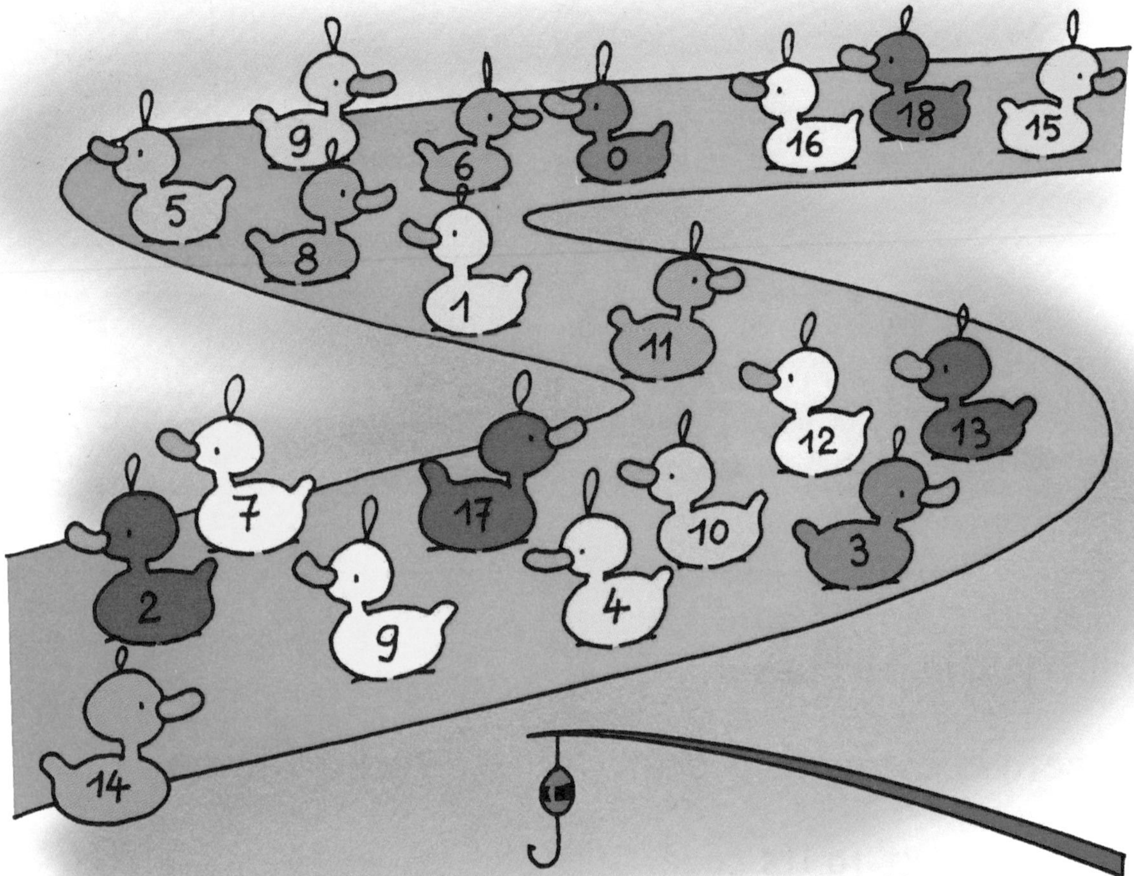
9
6
0
16
18
15
5
8
1
11
12
13
7
17
10
3
2
9
4
14

18 + 0 = 18

...... + ... = 18

...... + ... = 18

...... + ... = 18

...... + ... = 18

...... + ... = 18

...... + ... = 18

...... + ... = 18

...... + ... = 18

...... + ... = 18

Finish this line.

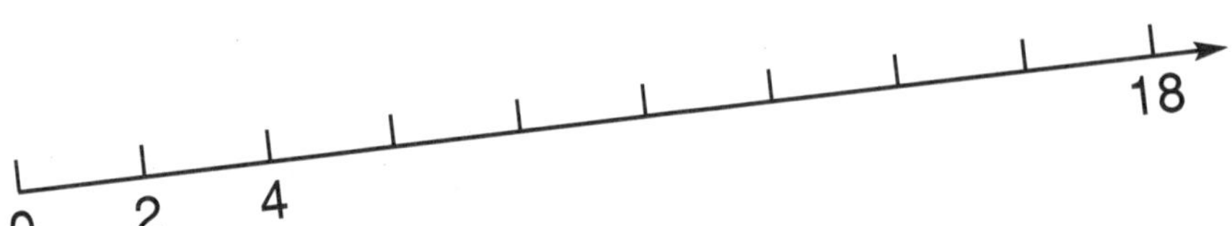
0
2
4
18

In each row, circle the sign
that matches the picture.

In each row, cross out the two numbers or letters that are different.

1	1	1	7	1	1	1	1	7
b	b	d	b	b	b	b	d	b
9	6	6	6	6	9	6	6	6
m	m	m	n	n	m	m	m	m
3	3	3	3	3	8	3	8	3
u	n	u	u	u	n	u	u	u
4	4	4	7	4	4	4	4	7
p	p	q	p	q	p	p	p	p
5	5	5	5	5	5	6	6	5
t	f	t	t	t	f	t	t	t

Circle the letters and underline the numbers in the box at right that match those in the box at left.

Ⓑ 8	R B D 9 8 3 O E B 8 B 3 E 2 C
6 ⓔ	e 6 h e 9 l g e 6 f d k o 6 b
Ⓖ 5	G g B 5 5 F S 3 8 Q D G 5 X J
Ⓟ 9	D 6 9 C P 5 3 O P V 9 P G C B 6 9

Connect the balls to the corresponding net.

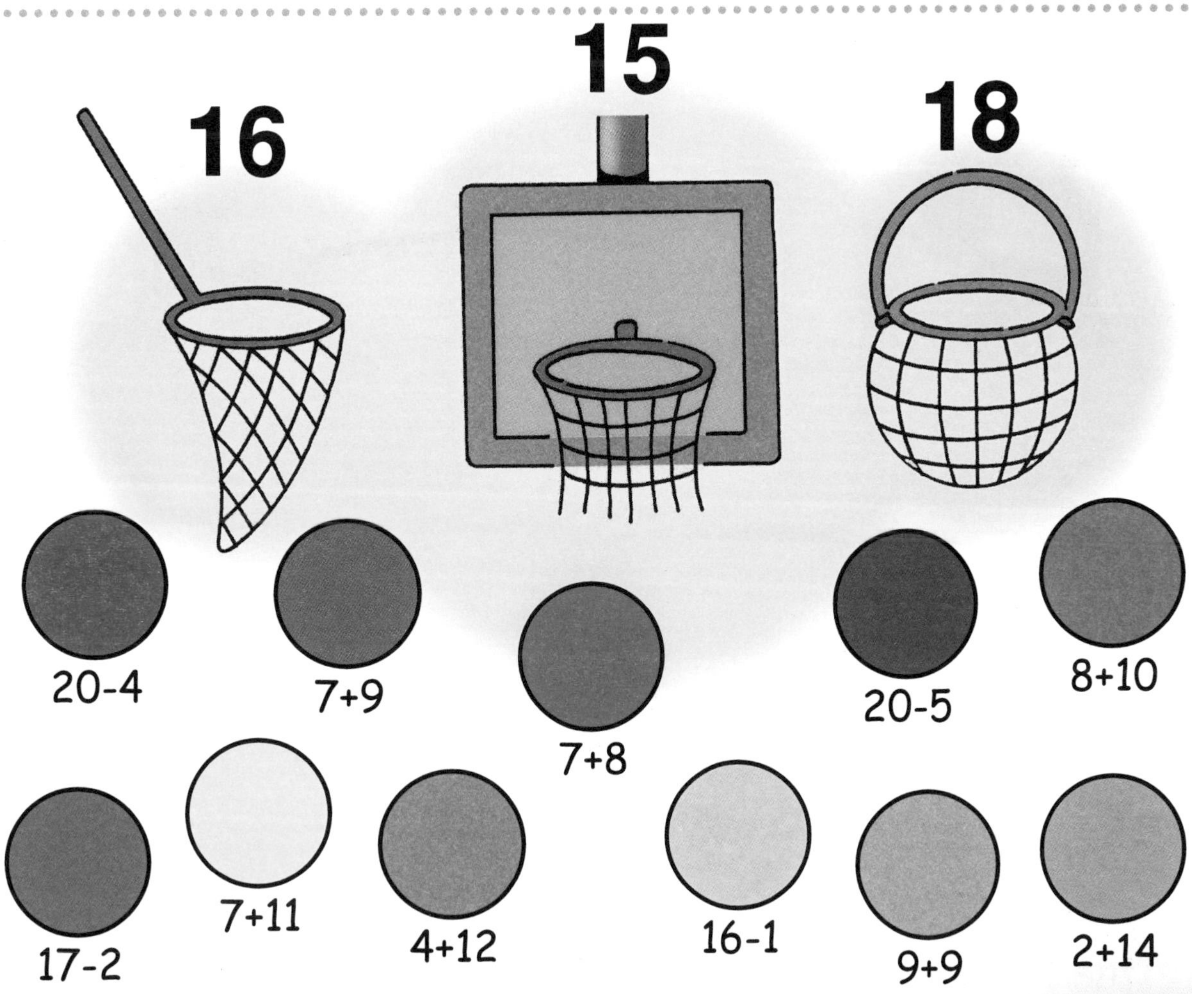
16
15
18
20-4
7+9
7+8
20-5
8+10
17-2
7+11
4+12
16-1
9+9
2+14

Connect the numbers from 1 to 20,
and you will see a figure you can color.

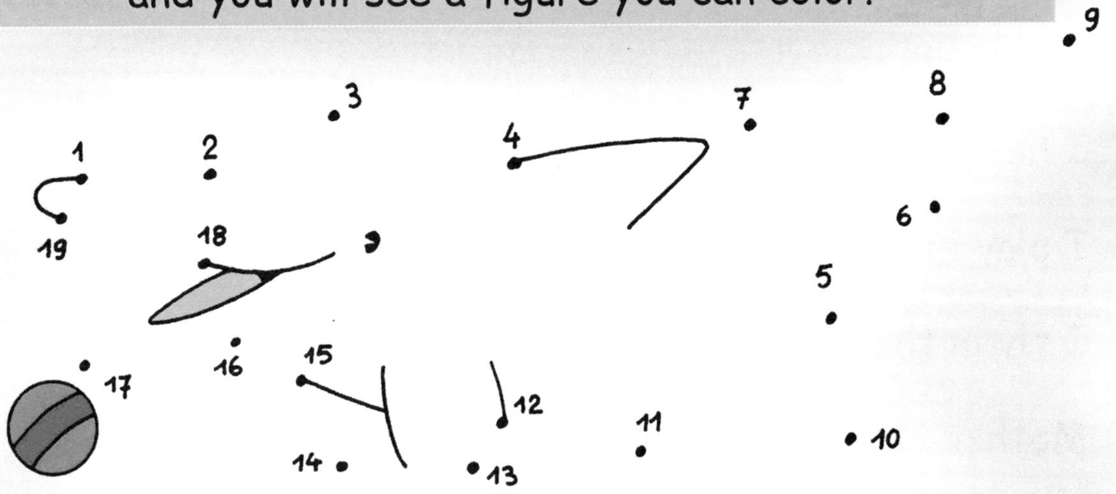
1
2
3
4
5
6
7
8
9
10
11
12
13
14
15
16
17
18
19

Some of the sentences below have errors in them. Underline the mistaken words and write the proper word in the right column. Do not modify the correct sentences!

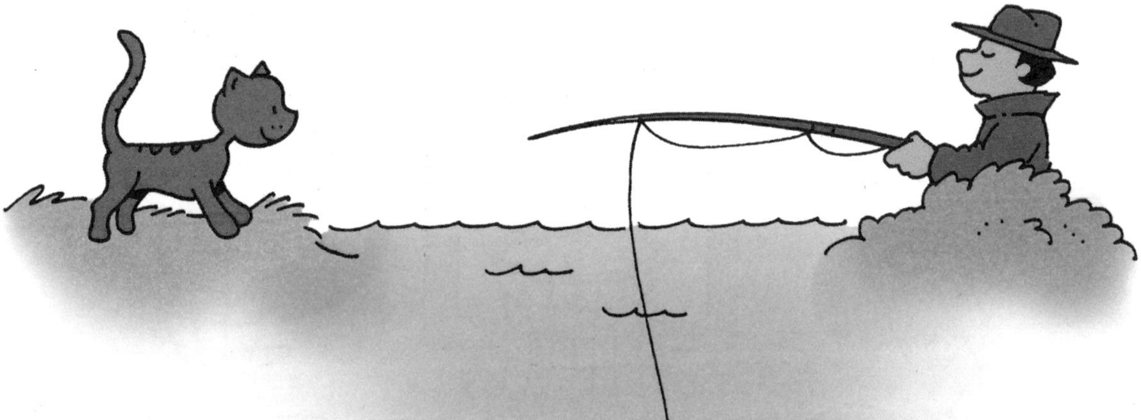

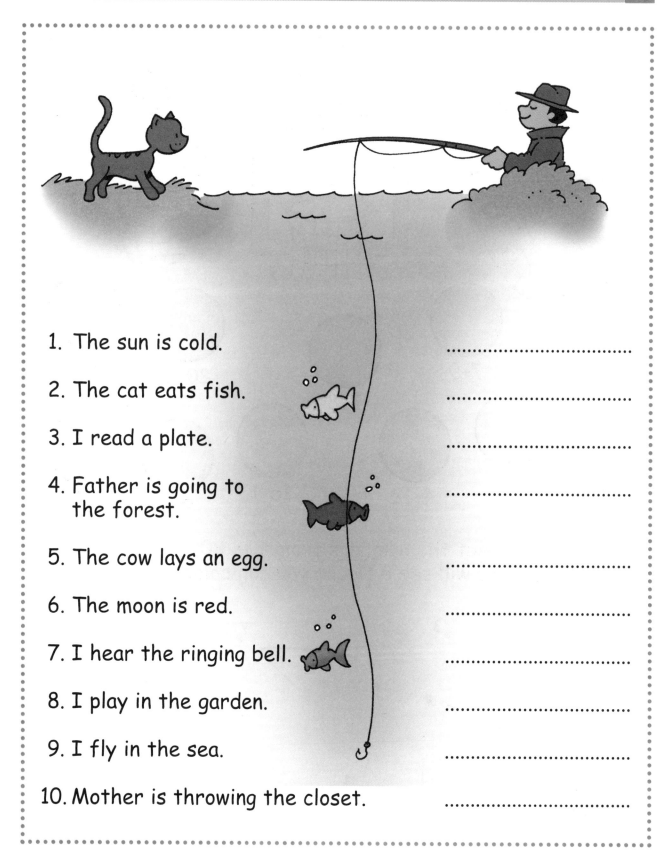

1. The sun is cold. ....
2. The cat eats fish. ....
3. I read a plate. ....
4. Father is going to the forest. ....
5. The cow lays an egg. ....
6. The moon is red. ....
7. I hear the ringing bell. ....
8. I play in the garden. ....
9. I fly in the sea. ....
10. Mother is throwing the closet. ....

Some drops are falling into each puddle.
For each add the number in the puddle with
the number in the drop and write the sum.

6
10

...... + ... = ...

7
8

...... + ... = ...

8
7

...... + ... = ...

3
3
12

...... + ... + ... = ...

3
9

...... + ... = ...

2
3
14

...... + ... + ... = ...

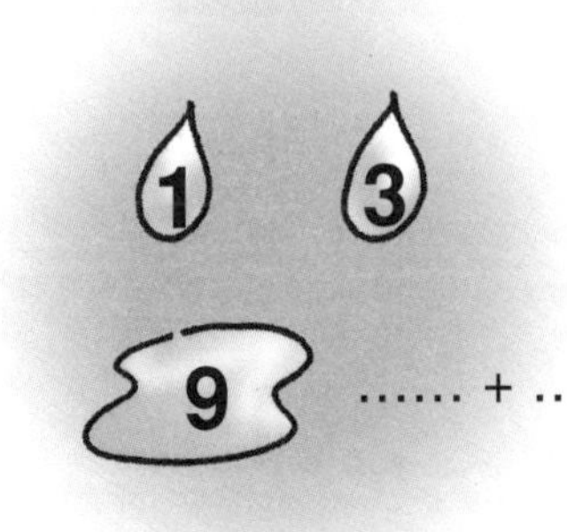
1
3
9

...... + ... + ... = ...

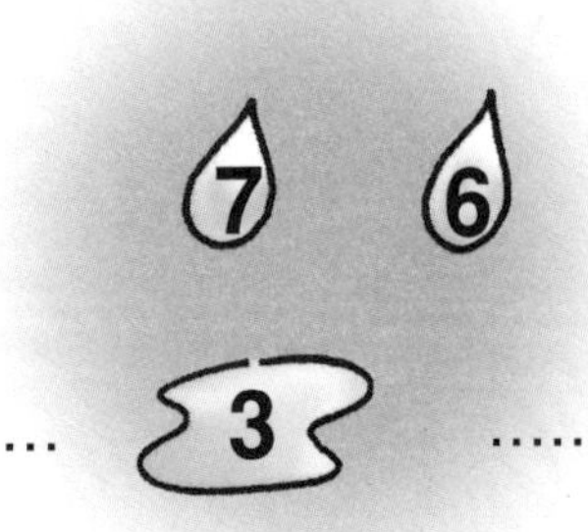
7
6
3

...... + ... + ... = ...

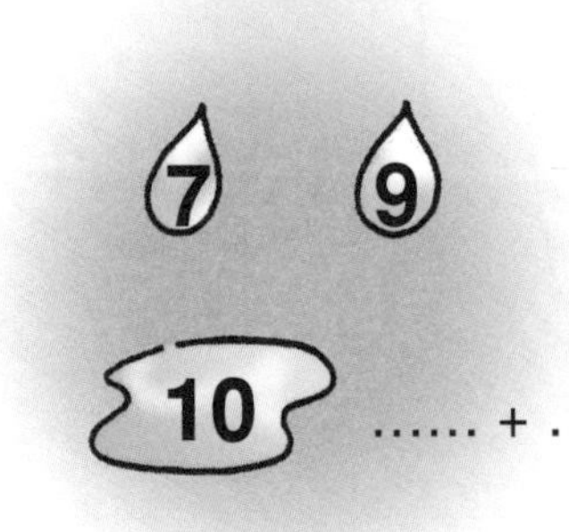
7
9
10

...... + ... + ... = ...

8
2
4

.... + ... + ... = ...

Draw an arrow from each addition or subtraction to the right sum.

12+2	10	1+9	18
10+2	14	1+12	13
8+2	8	1+15	10
6+2	12	1+17	16

20-3	12	16-4	13
16-3	13	8-4	5
19-3	17	9-4	4
15-3	16	17-4	12

6+5	14	20-6	14
9+5	11	17-6	3
12+5	19	9-6	11
14+5	17	11-6	5

Can you divide each number in two equal numbers?
Write these numbers in each cherry.

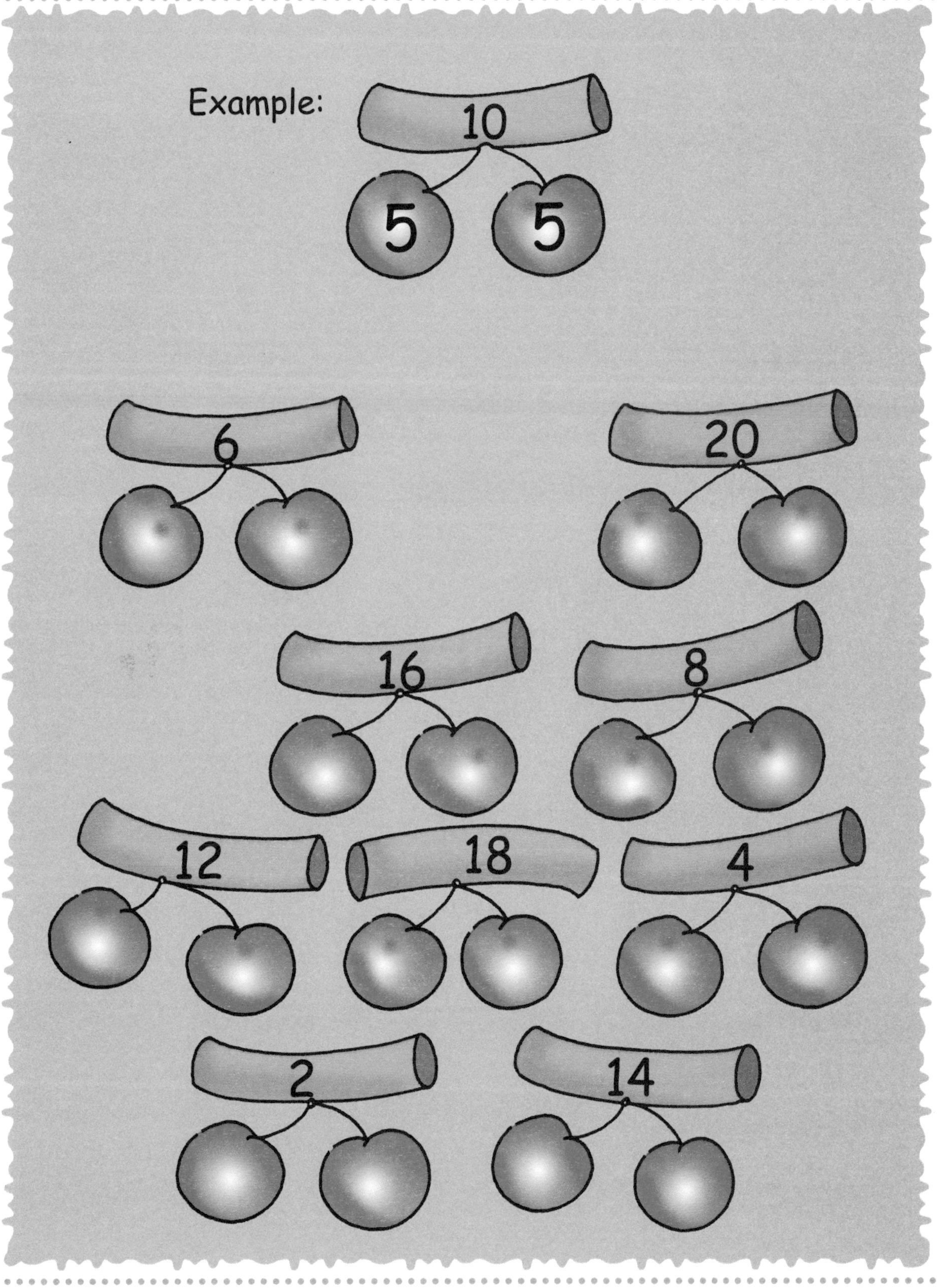
Example:
10
5
5
6
20
16
8
12
18
4
2
14

Match the pairs.

rake ○	○ school
hour ○	○ den
flower ○	○ garden
lesson ○	○ hen
bear ○	○ fire
egg ○	○ clock
candle ○	○ sock
foot ○	○ vase

---

pan ○	○ sight
lake ○	○ meat
branch ○	○ shore
eye ○	○ skeleton
stamp ○	○ letter
finger ○	○ tree
bone ○	○ grass
green ○	○ ring

Follow the arrow and add or subtract each of the numbers that is written next to the first arrow. Write the result on the dotted line.

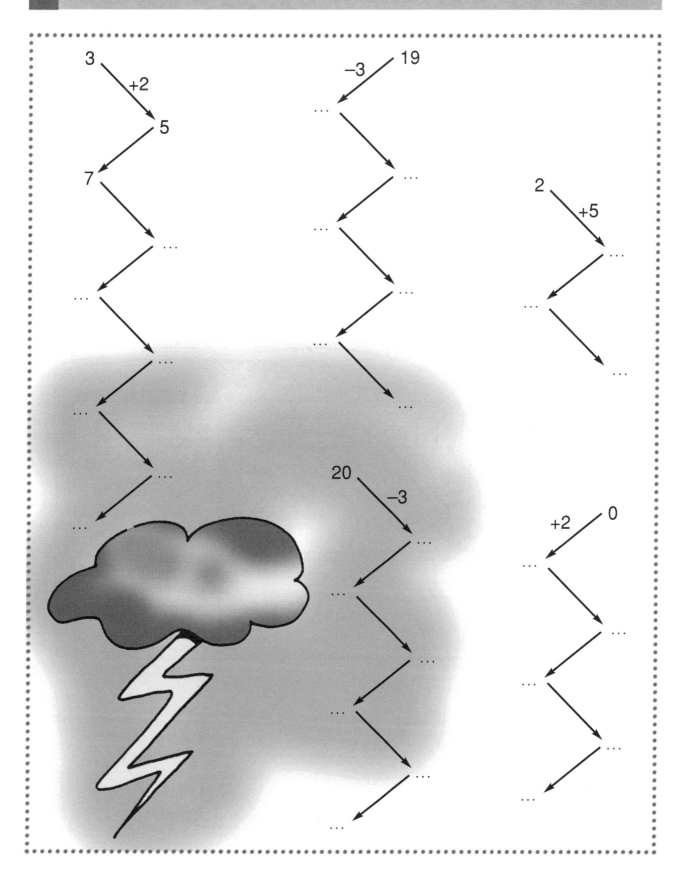

3 → +2 → 5 → 7 → … → … → … → … → … → …

19 → −3 → … → … → … → … → … → …

2 → +5 → … → … → …

20 → −3 → … → … → … → … → … → …

0 → +2 → … → … → … → … → … → …

Finish the rows of letters on the house.

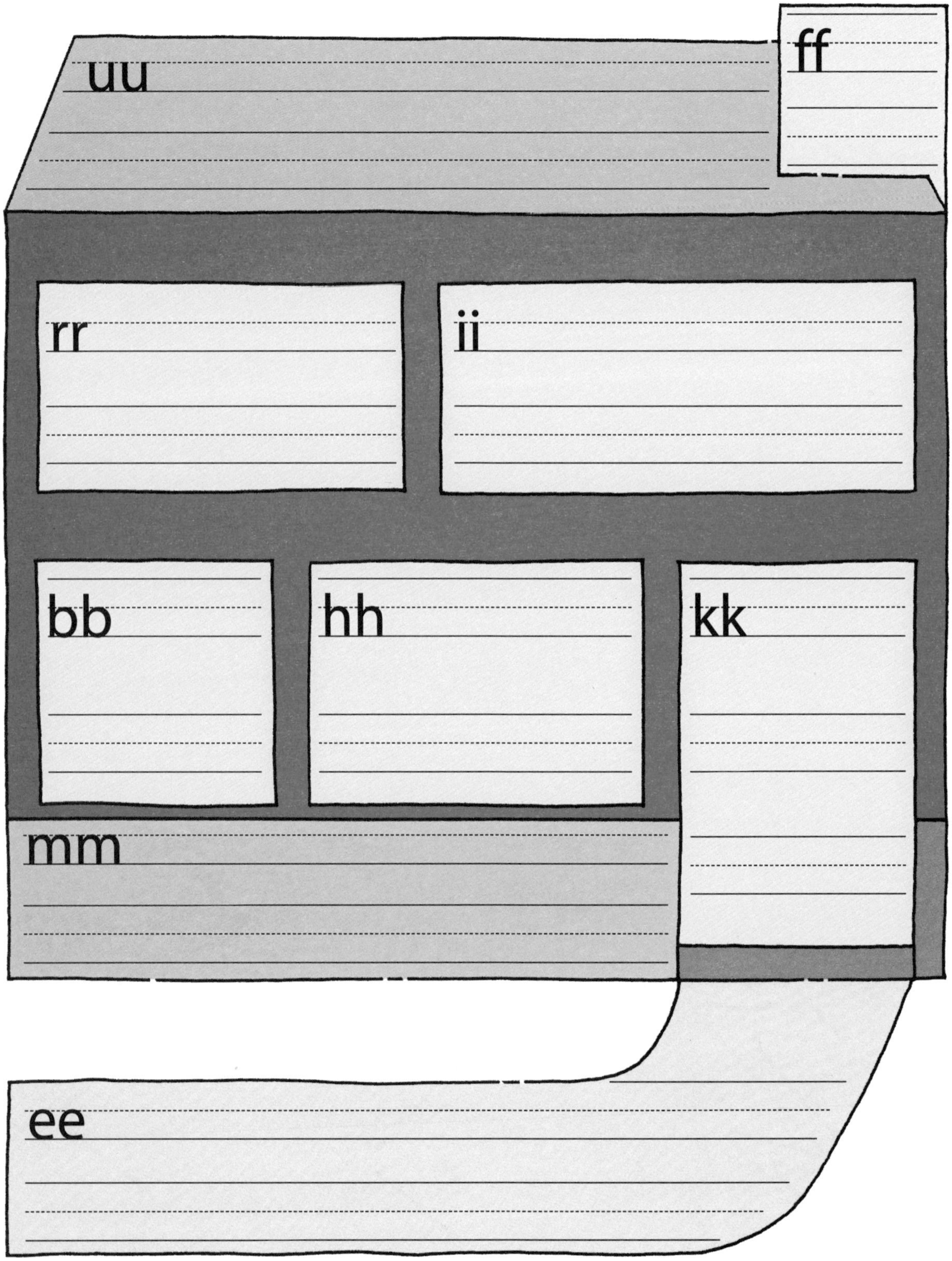
uu
ff
rr
ii
bb
hh
kk
mm
ee

Bubbles with numbers are escaping from these pipes. Solve the subtractions and write the solutions on the dotted lines.

Example:

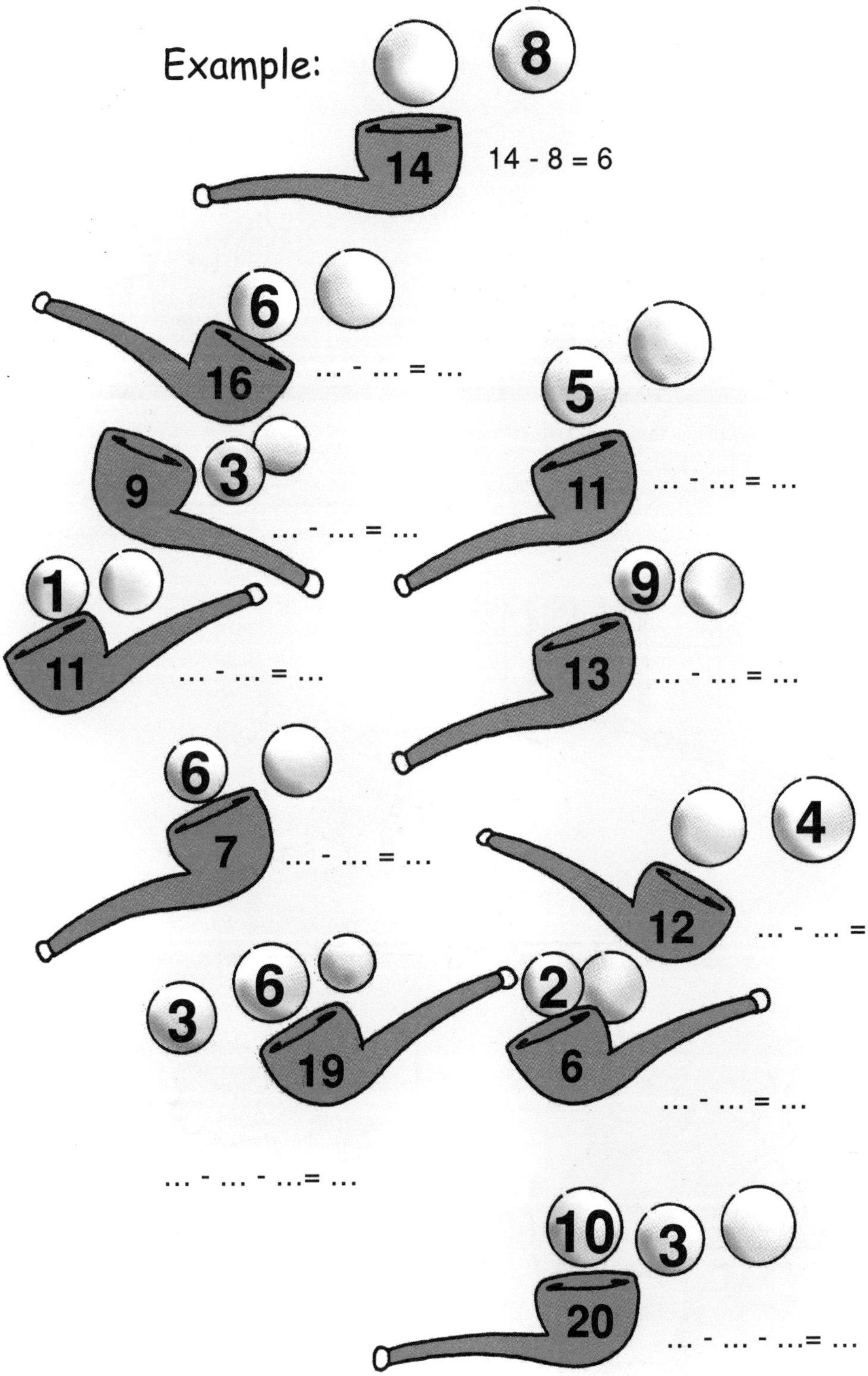
8
14
6
16
5
11
9
3
1
11
9
13
6
7
4
12
3
6
19
2
6
10
3
20

14 - 8 = 6

... - ... = ...

... - ... = ...

... - ... = ...

... - ... = ...

... - ... = ...

... - ... = ...

... - ... = ...

... - ... = ...

... - ... - ...= ...

... - ... - ...= ...

Write in each box the time of the day that corresponds to the action in the picture.

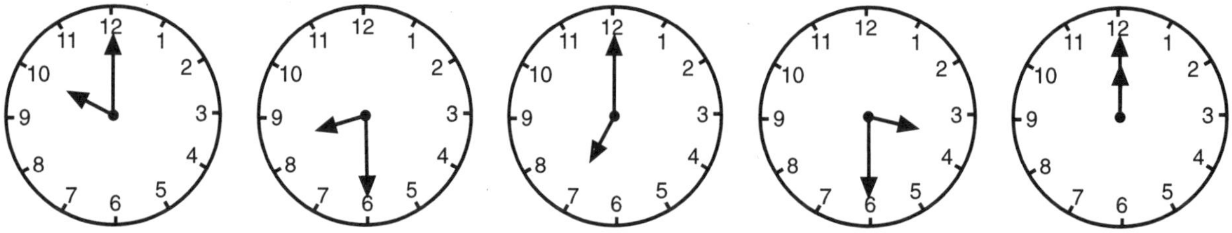

Fill the empty boxes so that the sum of the numbers on each of the three rows is the same.

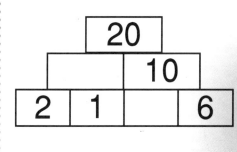

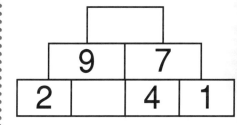

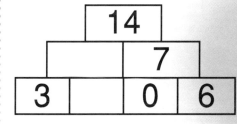

	20		
		10	
2	1		6

	18		
	6		
0	2		1

	9	7	
2		4	1

	15		
	8	7	
1		3	5

	14		
		7	
3		0	6

	12		
	10		
2	5		1

	19		
	8		
4	4		1

	5	5	
3	2	1	

Connect all the acceptable letters and parcels to the mailbox. Only the letters and parcels that have the value of 20 stamps are acceptable.

18
2
9
11
16
3
7
6
9
10
1
10
10
8
12
15
5
4
10
2
4
16

1. Circle the correct solution for each subtraction.
2. Complete these match problems with the = or ≠ sign.

1.

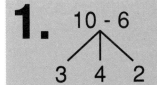

10 - 6 3 4 2	12 - 9 3 4 2	8 - 6 3 4 2	10 - 7 3 4 2
11 - 8 3 4 2	9 - 7 3 4 2	13 - 10 3 4 2	16 - 12 3 4 2
13 - 11 3 4 2	11 - 7 3 4 2	8 - 4 3 4 2	11 - 9 3 4 2

2.

10 + 2 .... 14 - 2
8 - 3 .... 15 -10
14 - 3 .... 18 - 6
7 + 6 .... 9 + 4
6 + 6 .... 20 - 8
9 - 8 .... 1 + 2
19 + 1 .... 20 - 0
8 + 8 .... 20 - 4
10 - 7 .... 0 + 6
5 + 8 .... 15 - 3

Write the first letter of the solution in the corresponding box. You will discover words in Susie's secret language.

4 + 5 = 9

5 + 6 = ...

20 - 4 = ...

2 + 8 = ...

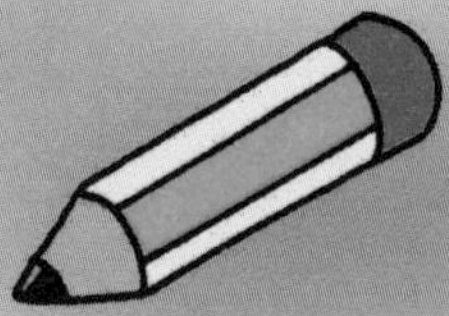

n			

18 - 5 = ...

7 - 6 = ...

3 + 16 = ...

5 + 6 = ...

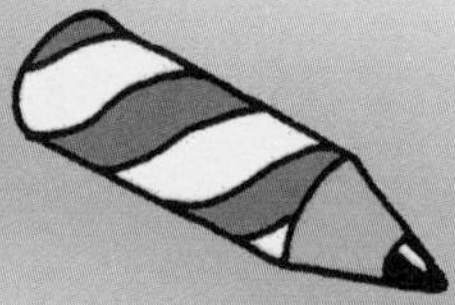

10 + 10 = ...

2 + 6 = ...

12 - 5 = ...

13 + 7 = ...

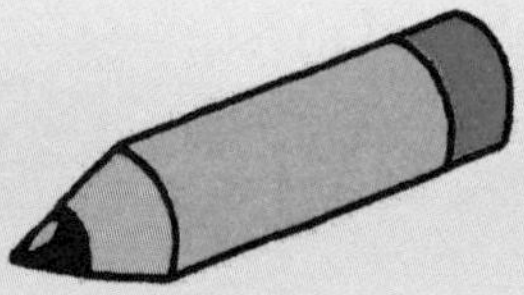

9 + 0 = ...

14 - 13 = ...

18 - 8 = ...

6 + 12 = ...

Count the empty boxes and the shaded ones separately. Then add the two numbers.

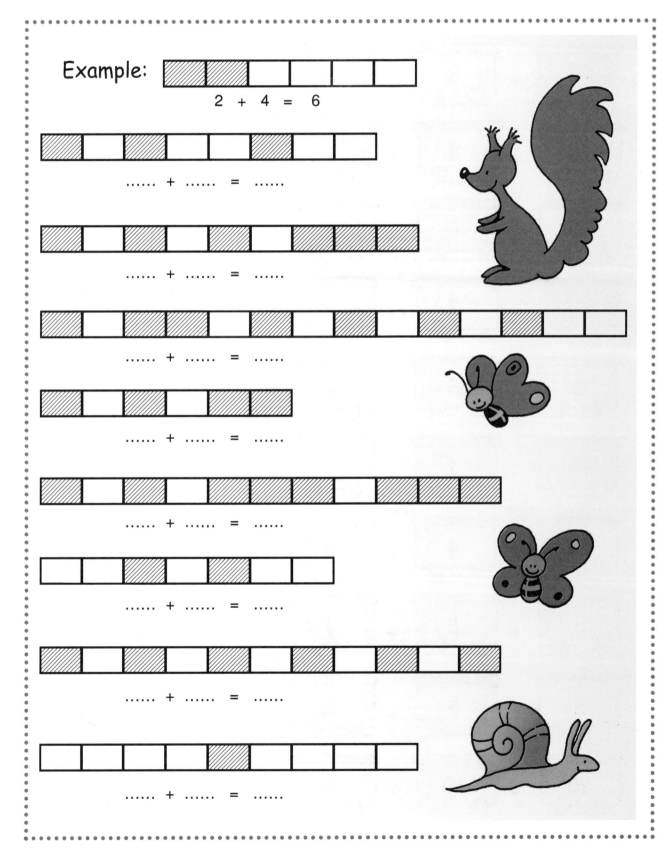

Example: 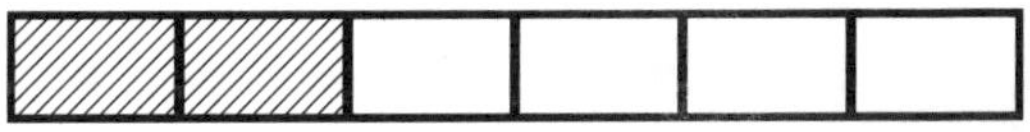

2 + 4 = 6

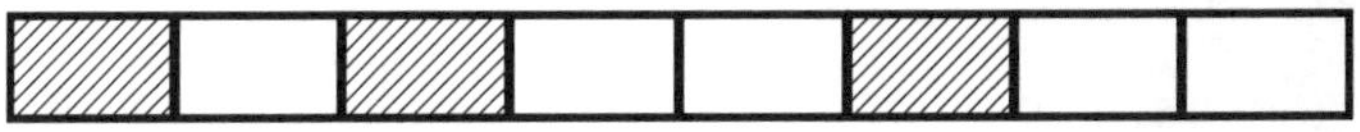

...... + ... = ...

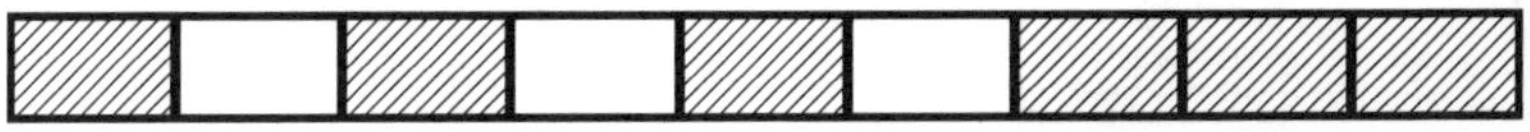

...... + ... = ...

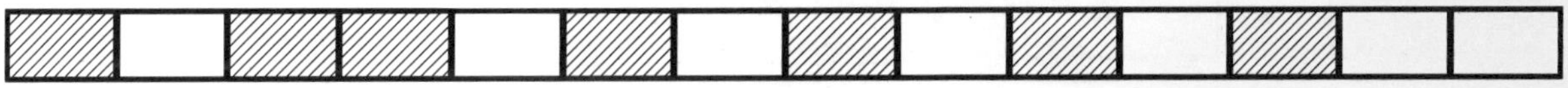

...... + ... = ...

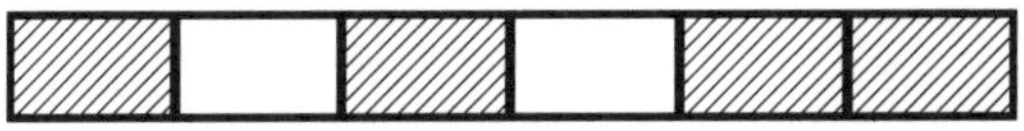

...... + ... = ...

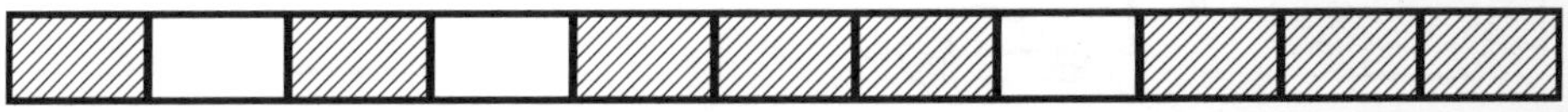

...... + ... = ...

...... + ... = ...

...... + ... = ...

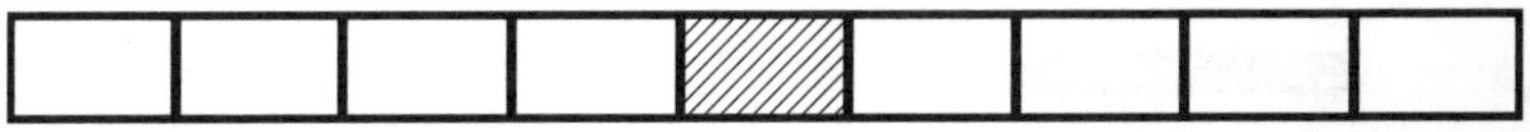

...... + ... = ...

These coaches belong to which engine? Connect them.

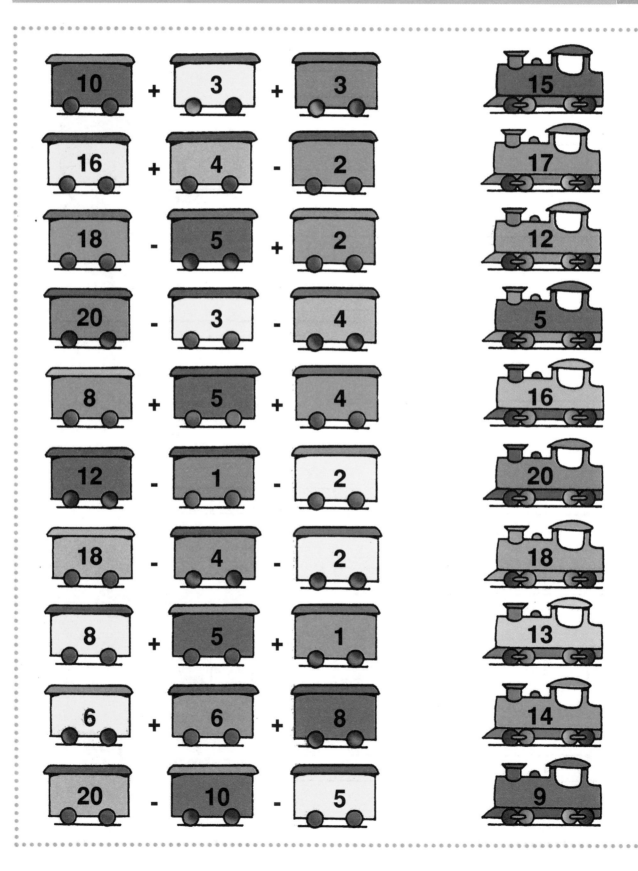

Coaches	Engines
10 + 3 + 3	15
16 + 4 - 2	17
18 - 5 + 2	12
20 - 3 - 4	5
8 + 5 + 4	16
12 - 1 - 2	20
18 - 4 - 2	18
8 + 5 + 1	13
6 + 6 + 8	14
20 - 10 - 5	9

Read each sentence carefully and circle the proper word.

1. The horse is — mad / lad

2. On the lake I see a — goat / boat

3. Jack is sleeping — late / mate

4. The weather is — mine / fine

5. His hair is — red / mad

6. The mountain is — fig / big

7. I live in a beautiful — house / mouse

8. I would like to eat a — peach / beach

9. She is cooking — meat / meet

10. Mary is reading a — book / look

Add the following numbers.

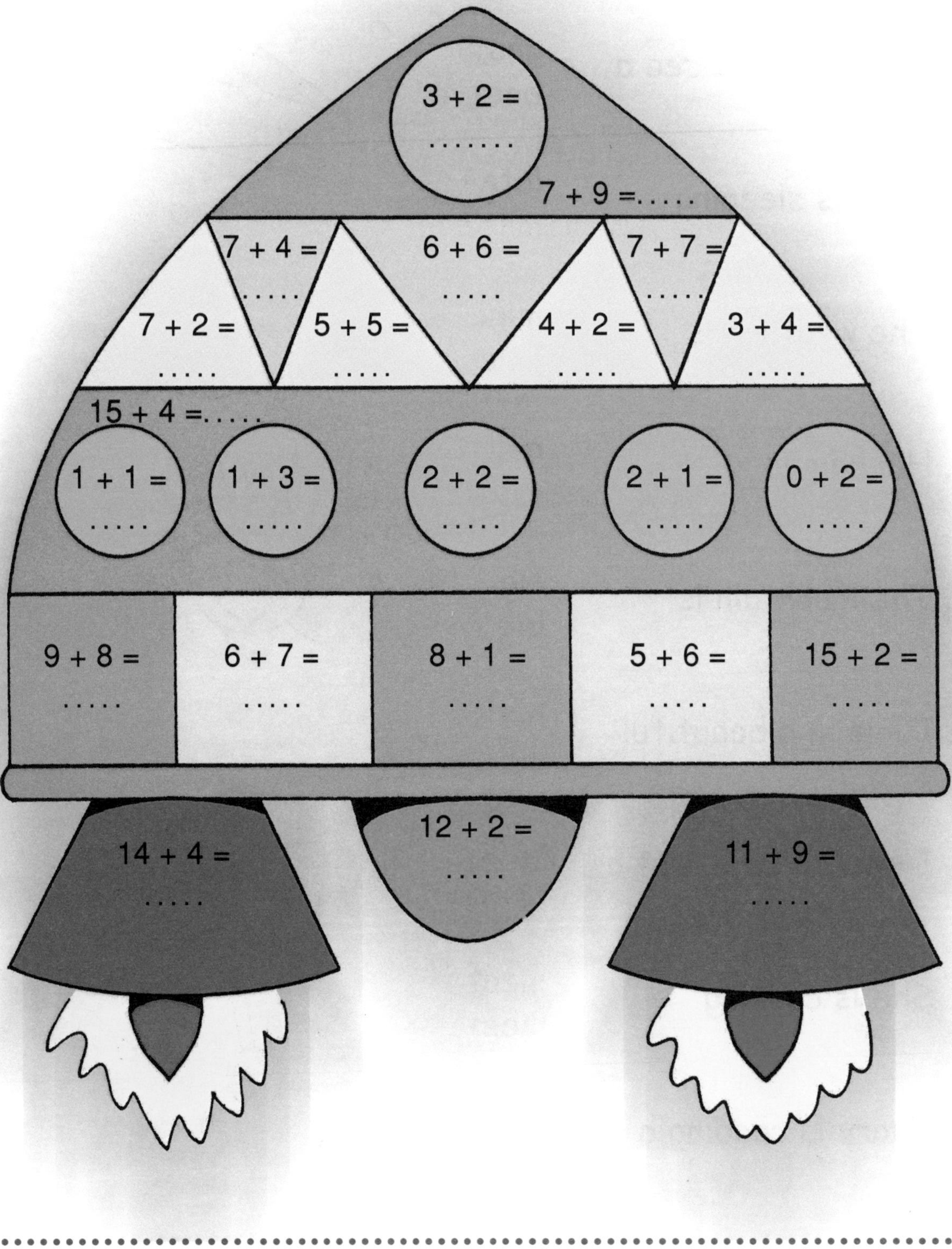
3 + 2 =
....
7 + 9 =.....
7 + 4 =
.....
6 + 6 =
.....
7 + 7 =
.....
7 + 2 =
.....
5 + 5 =
.....
4 + 2 =
.....
3 + 4 =
.....
15 + 4 =.....
1 + 1 =
.....
1 + 3 =
.....
2 + 2 =
.....
2 + 1 =
.....
0 + 2 =
.....
9 + 8 =
.....
6 + 7 =
.....
8 + 1 =
.....
5 + 6 =
.....
15 + 2 =
.....
14 + 4 =
.....
12 + 2 =
.....
11 + 9 =
.....

Five children put in or withdraw money from their piggy banks. Write the right amount in the circle. Look carefully at the direction indicated by the arrows. Write the total in the big circle. In the end who has the greatest sum of a money in his piggy bank?

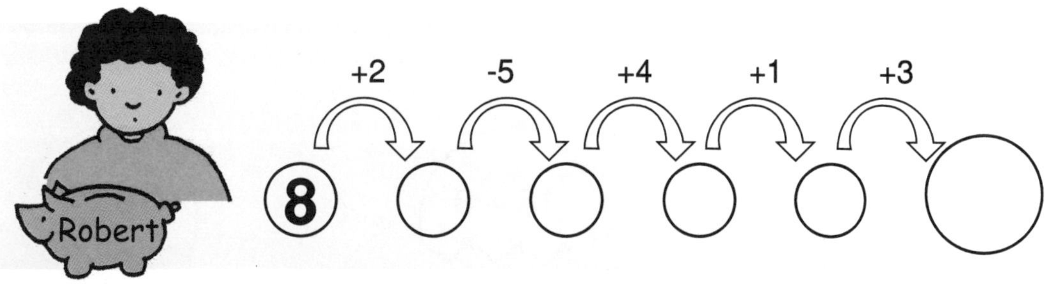
Robert
8
+2
-5
+4
+1
+3

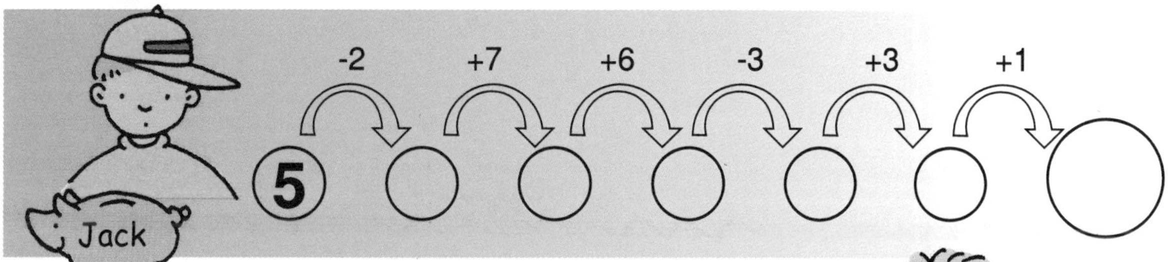
Jack
5
-2
+7
+6
-3
+3
+1

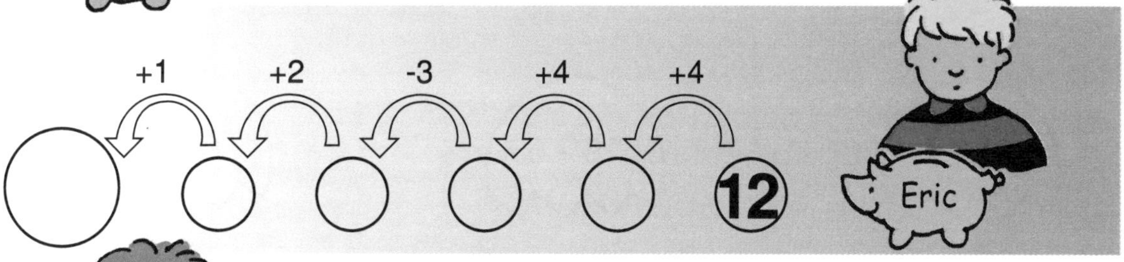
Eric
12
+1
+2
-3
+4
+4

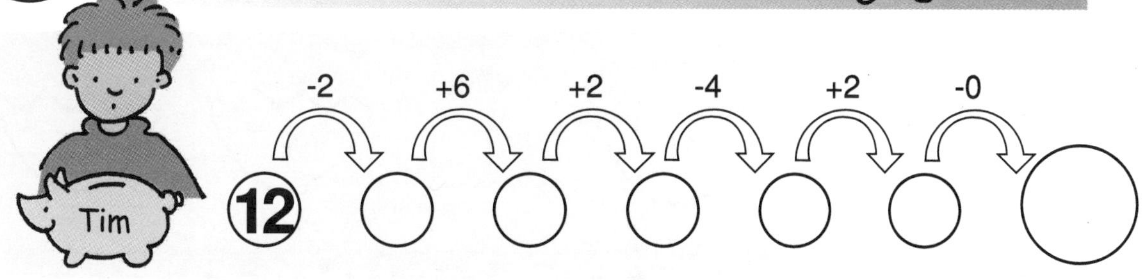
Tim
12
-2
+6
+2
-4
+2
-0

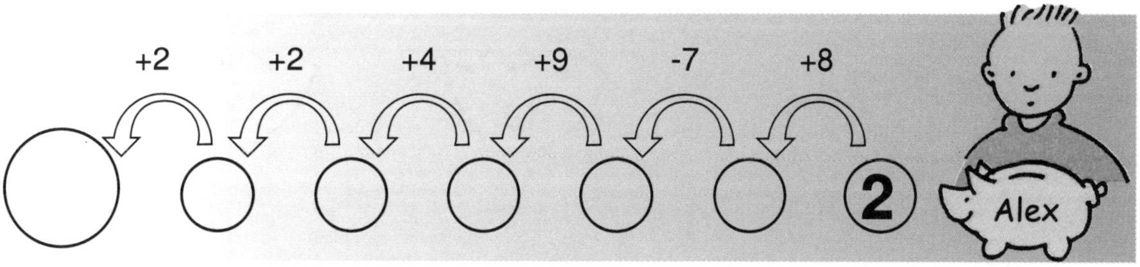
Alex
2
+2
+2
+4
+9
-7
+8

How much money is in each piggy bank?
Circle the name of the person who has the greatest sum.

Robert = ... Jack = ... Eric = ... Tim = ... Alex = ...

Connect the two halves of each egg. If you solve each math problem, you will find the two halves that form a whole egg. Color the two halves with the same color.

20 - 2 16 + 3 16 - 4

13 - 7 2 + 5 18 - 17 3 + 6

11 - 7 19 - 6 8 + 3

6 18 1 12

7 19 4

13 11 9

The teacher is playing skittles with her pupils.
Each pupil gets one turn. Figure out the points.
Only the knocked-over skittles may be counted.
Who is winning? Who is losing?

3
6
2
8
10

Ann: ....

10
2
8
3
6

Dana: ....

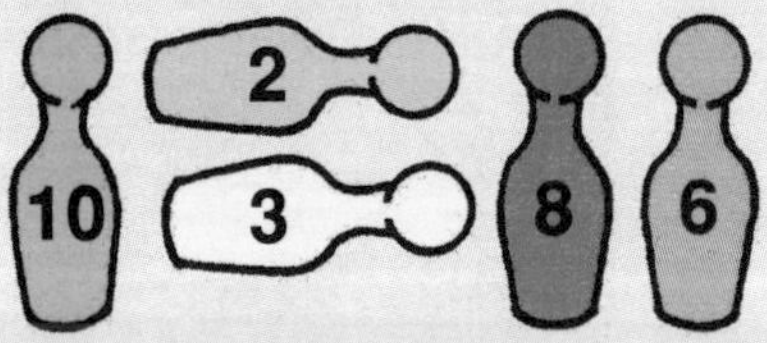
10
2
3
8
6

Paul: ....

8
2
6
3
10

Timmy: ....

8
3
10
6
2

Mary: ....

8
10
2
3
6

Sam: ....

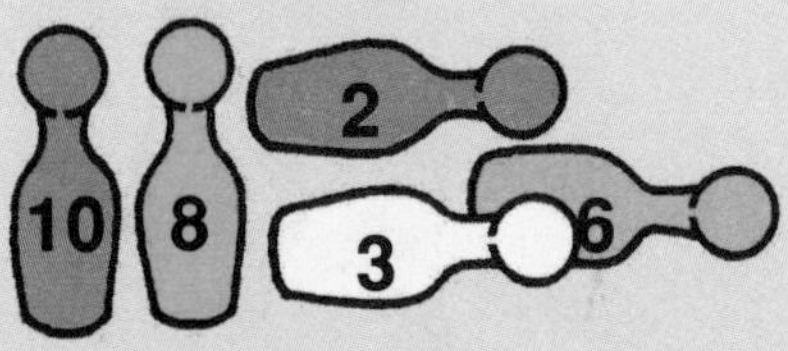
10
8
2
3
6

Jack: ....

10
8
2
6
3

Bill: ....

3
10
8
2
6

Susan: ....

8
10
3
2
6

Eric: ....

.... is winning and .... is losing.

Solve all of the subtraction and addition problems.
After you have the results, change the numbers
to letters. Form a sentence with these letters.
Read this sentence from top to bottom.

R = 14	S = 12	A = 10
H = 6	E = 11	D = 9
O = 18	B = 13	K = 15

Read

8 - 2 = ... = ...
19 - 8 = ... = ...

17 - 3 = ... = ...
8 + 3 = ... = ...
36 - 26 = ... = ...
16 - 7 = ... = ...
20 - 8 = ... = ...

20 - 10 = ... = ...

39 - 26 = ... = ...
36 - 18 = ... = ...
11 + 7 = ... = ...
12 + 3 = ... = ...

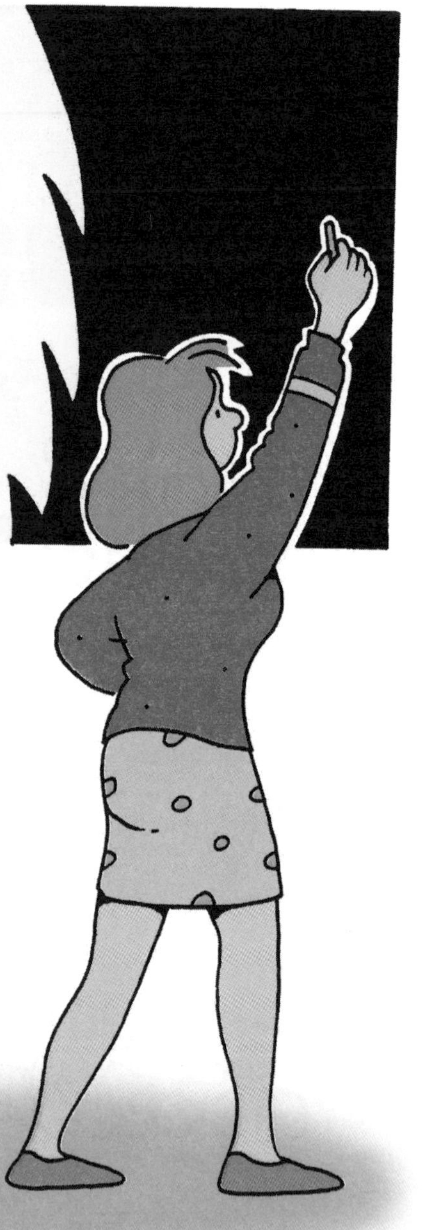

Write the sentence here.

....

Circle the correct sentence under each picture.

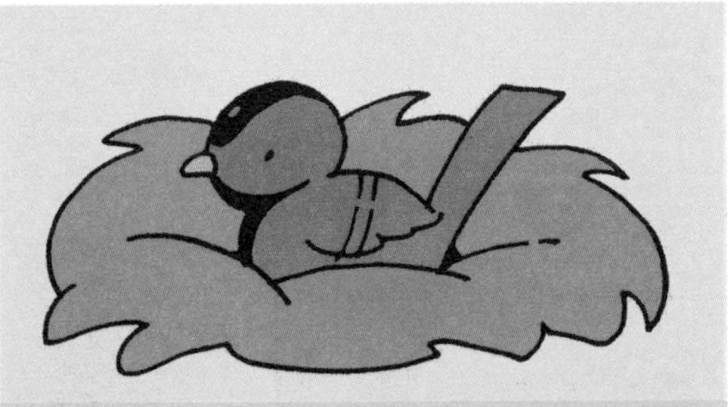

The bird is on its nest.

The bird is in front of its nest.

The bird is in its nest.

Jack is on the fence.

Jack is at the left side of the fence.

Jack is in front of the fence.

Eric is at the farmer.

Eric is on the farmer.

Eric is in front of the farmer

The raven eats the cheese.

The fox eats the cheese.

The fox eats the raven.

The cow is on the pen.

The cow is in front of the pen.

The cow is in the pen.

The cloud comes in front of the Sun.

The Sun comes in front of the cloud.

The cloud comes near the Sun.

Can you solve these problems by filling in the missing number?

- 14 = ... + 7
- 10 = ... + 1
- 18 = ... + 6
- 15 = ... + 8
- 20 = ... + 2
- 9 = ... + 5
- 17 = ... + 10
- 19 = ... + 12
- 16 = ... + 14

- 16 = ... - 3
- 17 = ... - 1
- 10 = ... - 10
- 15 = ... - 5
- 12 = ... - 7
- 9 = ... - 6
- 14 = ... - 2
- 8 = ... - 11
- 11 = ... - 9

Can you form a word with the letters on each plate?
It is not necessary to use all of the letters.

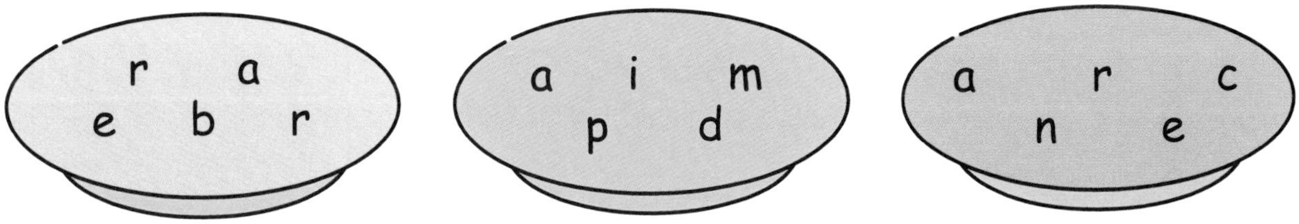
r a e b r
a i m p d
a r c n e

....

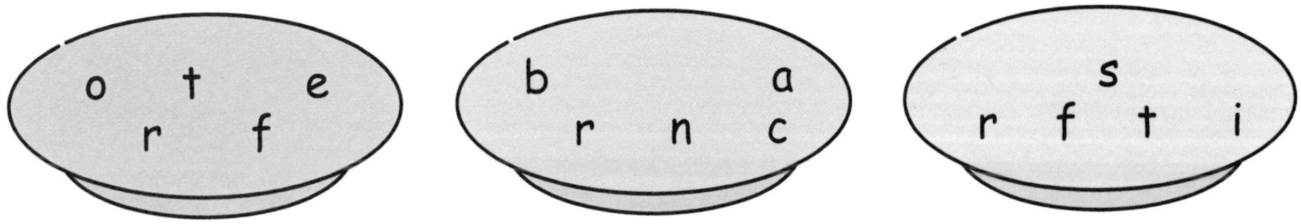
o t e r f
b a r n c
s r f t i

....

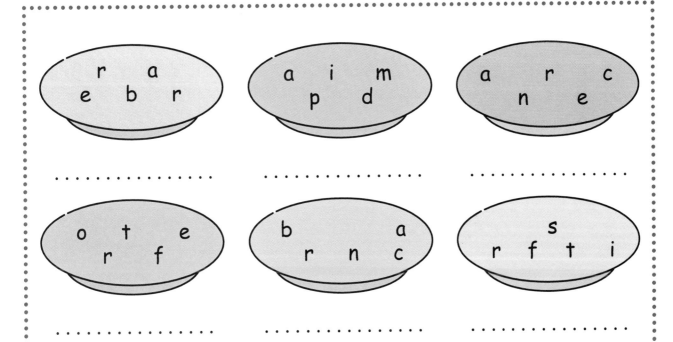

Use some of the following letters to form 5 different words. You can use the letters more than once.

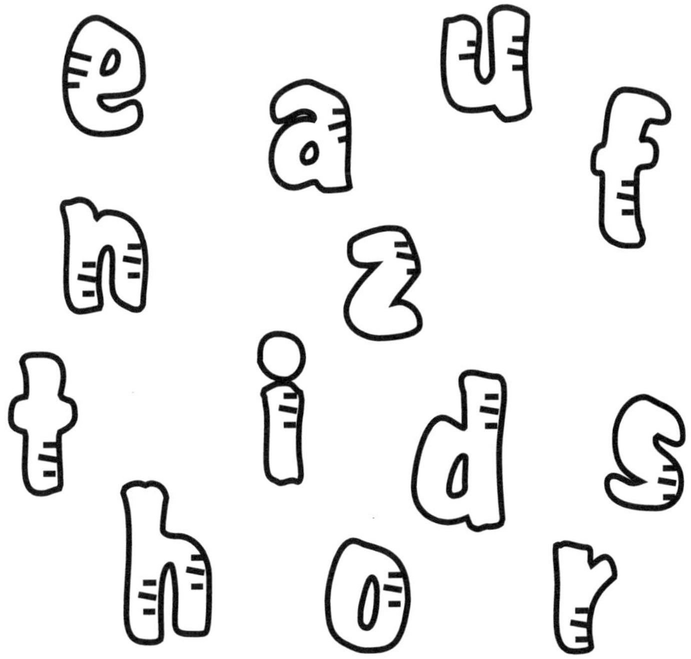
e a u f n z t i d s h o r

- ....
- ....
- ....
- ....
- ....

Solve the problems in the following grids.

-	1	2	3	4
5				
6				
7				
8				

+	2	4	6	8
2				
4				
6				
8				

+	2	5	8	6
3				
9				
10				
7				

-	9	10	7	5
18				
15				
10				
12				

-	12	8	11	6
20				
16				
19				
13				

+	11	9	13	4
5				
7				
2				
0				

Place these bricks in their proper order to make a sentence. Write the sentences on the dotted lines.

	the
journal	reads
	father

....

an	eat
I	apple

....

	nest	
flies	the	over
	its	
	sparrow	

....

dinner		
	mother	
	the	cooks

....

ball	runs
my	the
on	grass

....

five	Alex	has
	books	

....

in	sky	the
planes	I	see

....

ride	Jack	a	
	horse	wants	to

....

Complete each row with a card.
Each time the total must be 20.

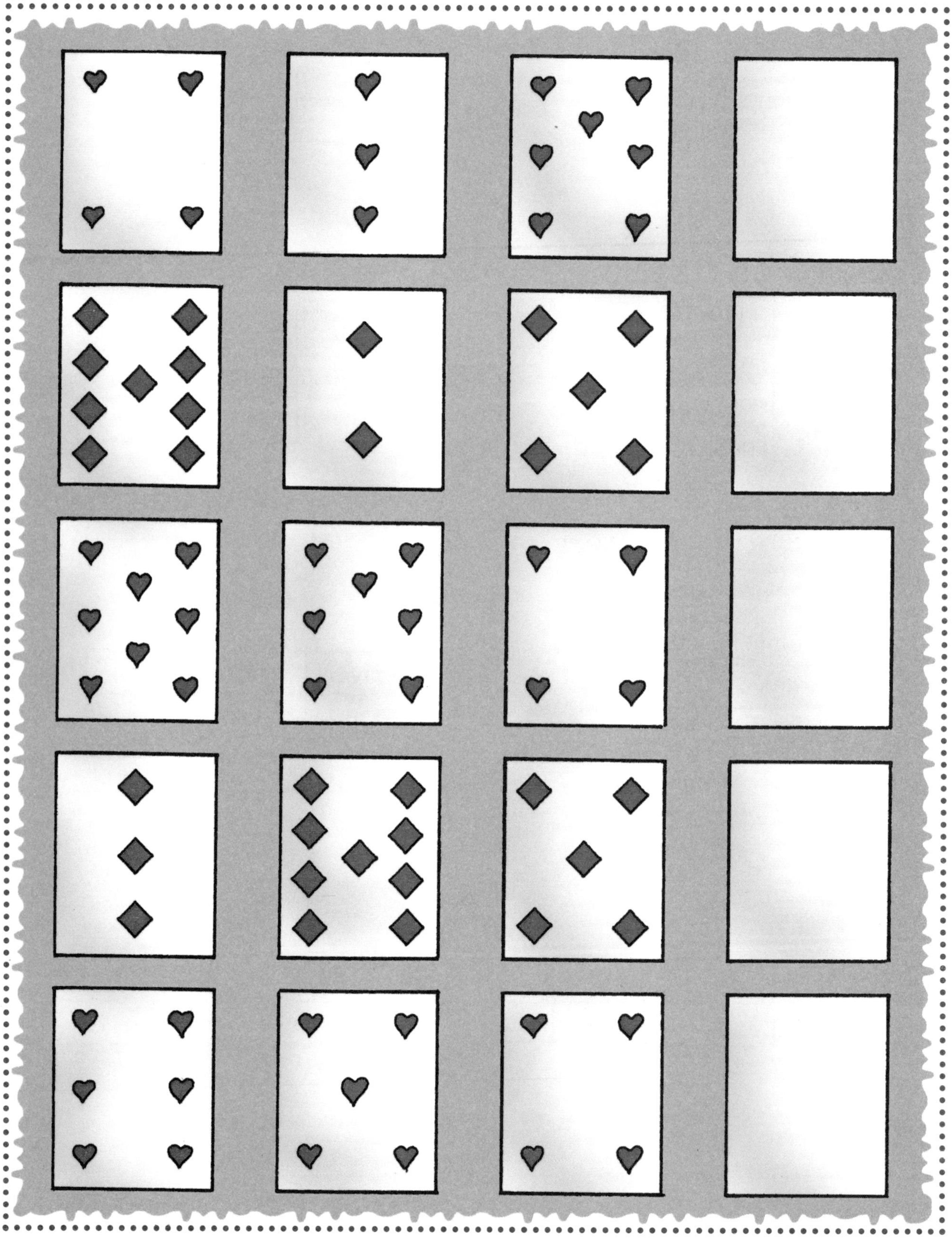

Read each phrase carefully and draw the clock hands in their proper places.

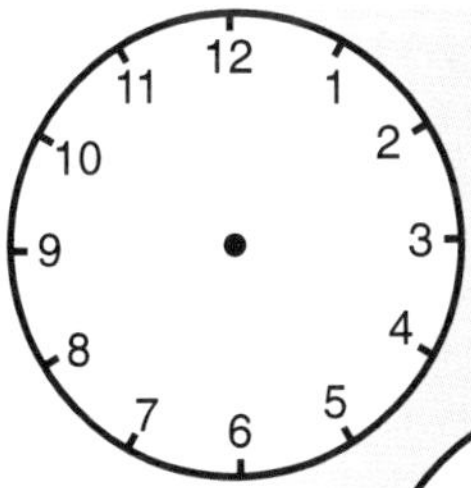
12
1
2
3
4
5
6
7
8
9
10
11

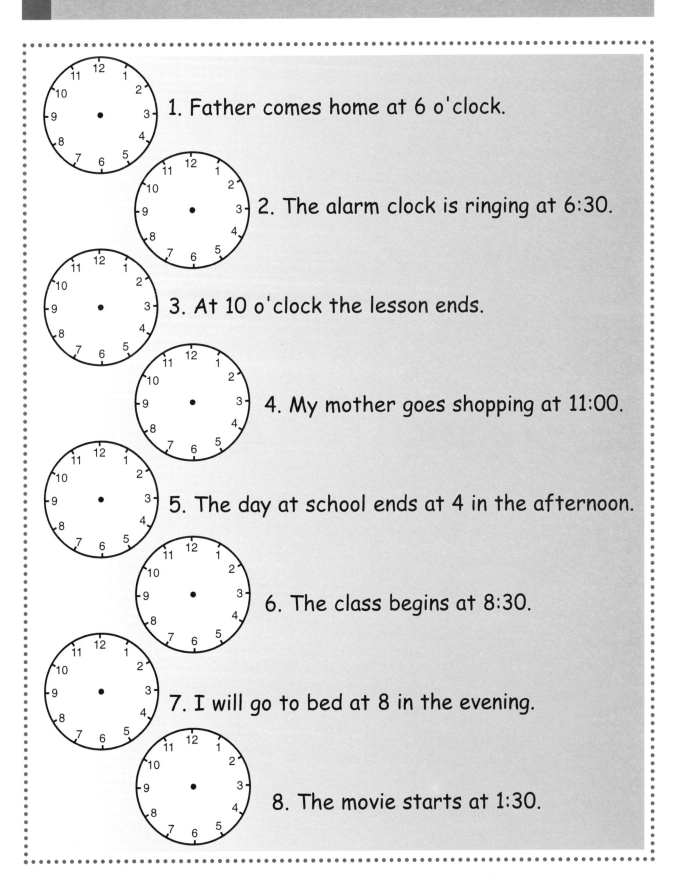

1. Father comes home at 6 o'clock.

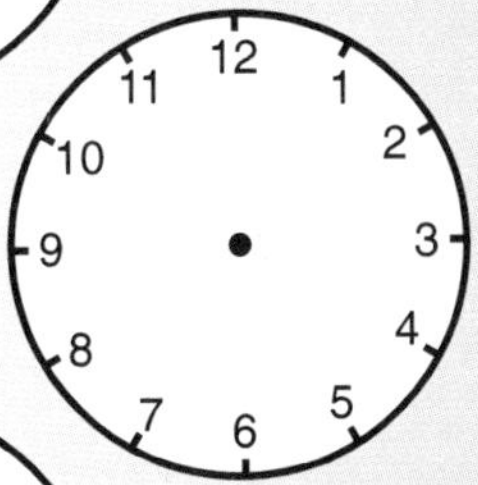
12
1
2
3
4
5
6
7
8
9
10
11

2. The alarm clock is ringing at 6:30.

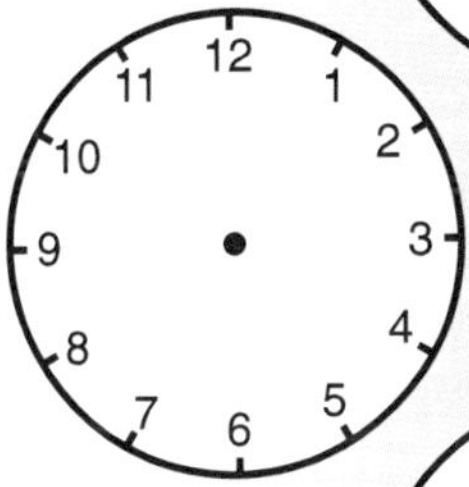
12
1
2
3
4
5
6
7
8
9
10
11

3. At 10 o'clock the lesson ends.

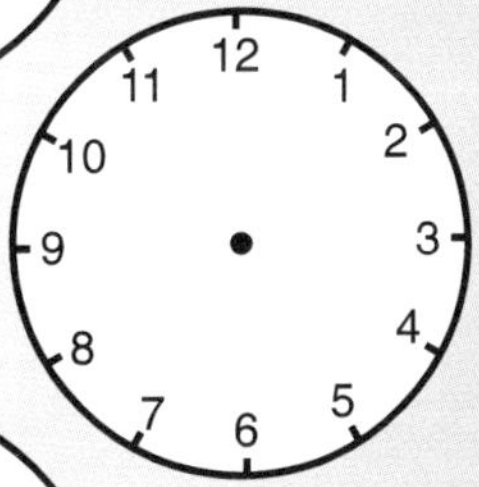
12
1
2
3
4
5
6
7
8
9
10
11

4. My mother goes shopping at 11:00.

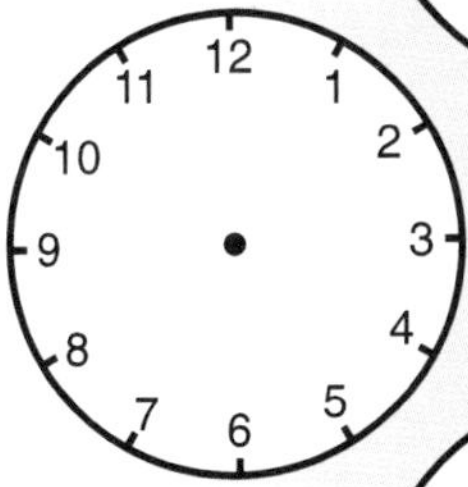
12
1
2
3
4
5
6
7
8
9
10
11

5. The day at school ends at 4 in the afternoon.

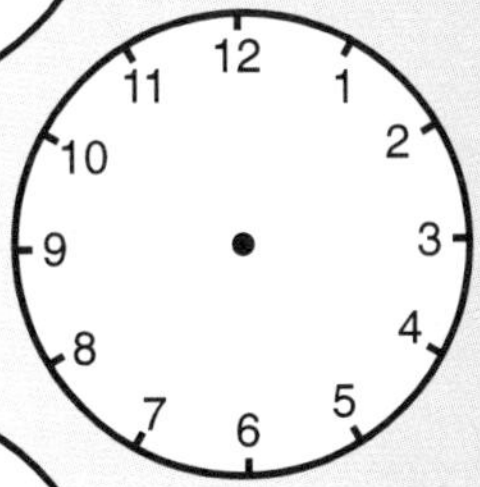
12
1
2
3
4
5
6
7
8
9
10
11

6. The class begins at 8:30.

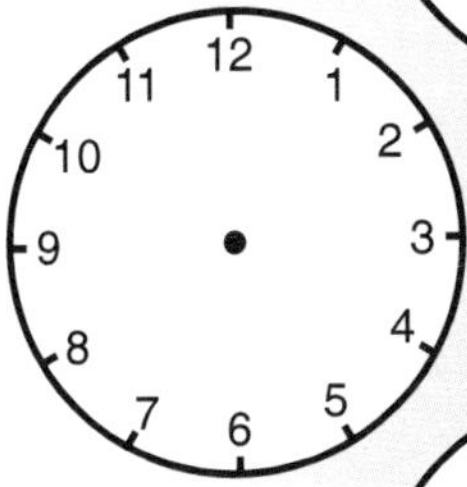
12
1
2
3
4
5
6
7
8
9
10
11

7. I will go to bed at 8 in the evening.

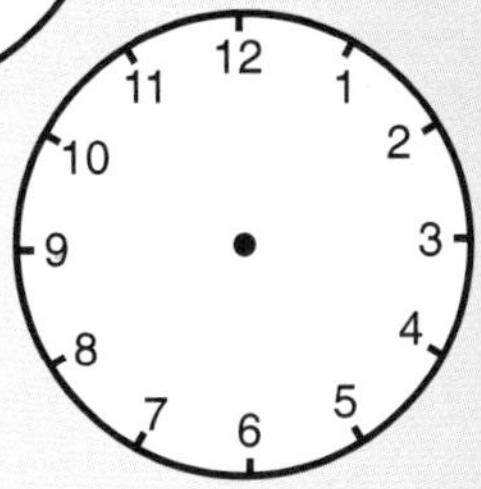
12
1
2
3
4
5
6
7
8
9
10
11

8. The movie starts at 1:30.

Six kids have bought goodies and paid for them with points. Calculate the number of points each kid has had to spend.

7 points

3 points

4 points

2 points

10 points

6 points

Jack: .... points

Alex: .... points

Eric: .... points

Dan: .... points

Timmy: .... points

Bill: .... points

All these objects may be used to write or draw. Write under each object its name. You can look in the table at the bottom of the page.

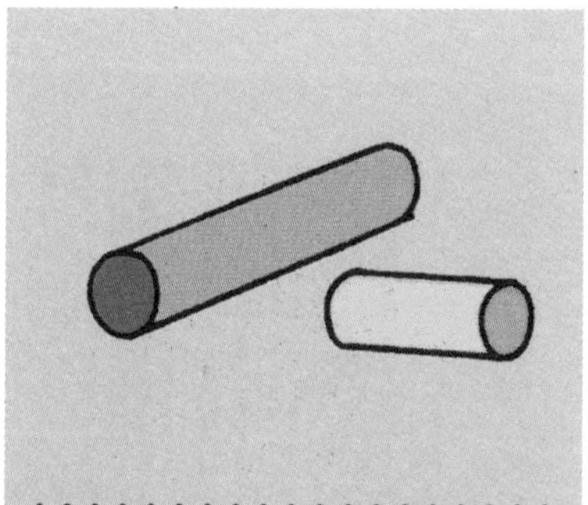

....

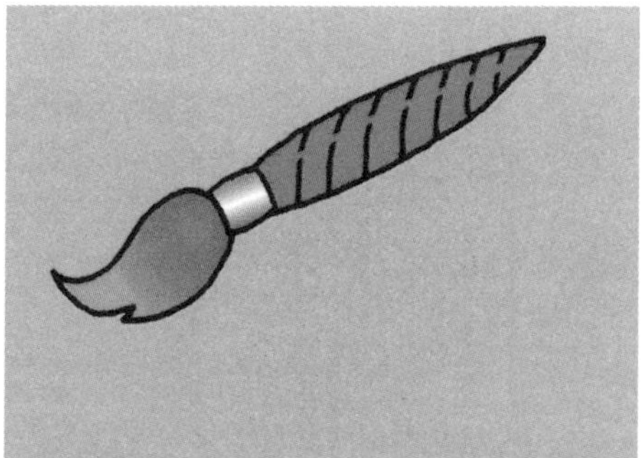

....

....

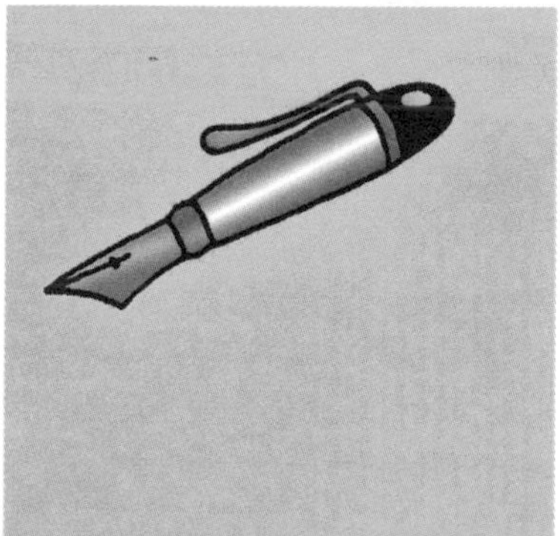

....

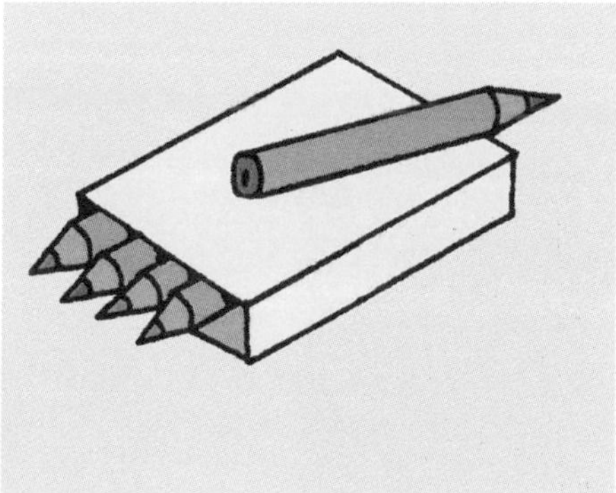

....

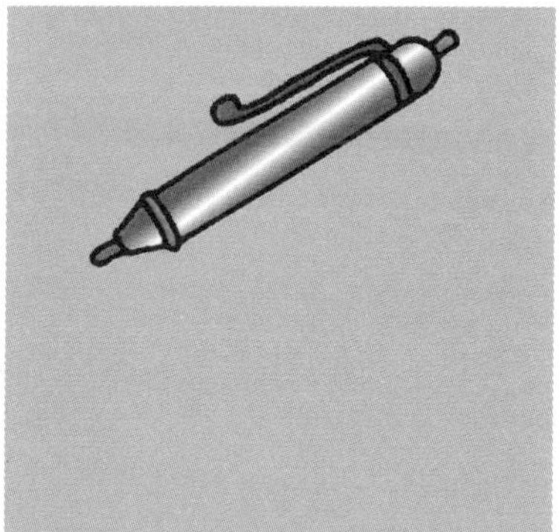

....

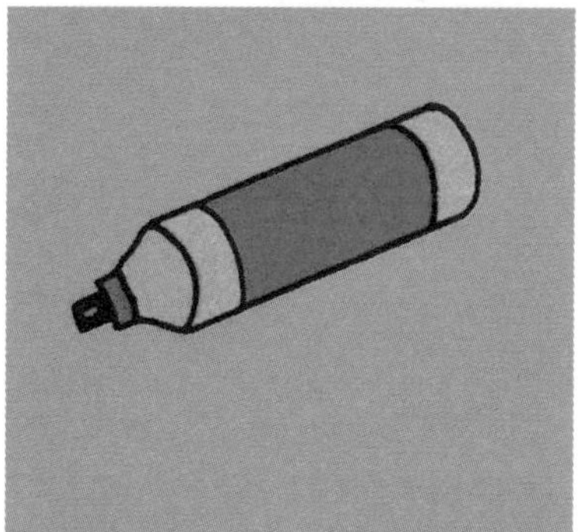

....

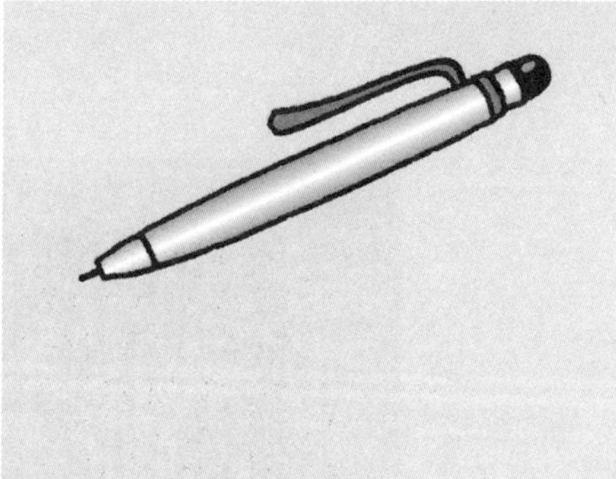

....

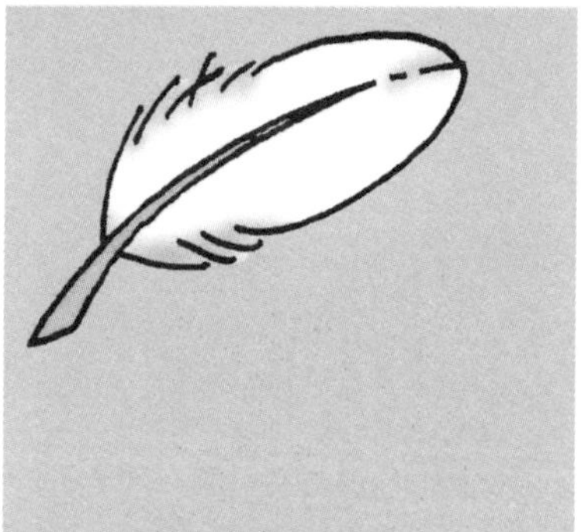

....

chalk	brush	pencil	fountain pen	crayons
ball point pen	felt tip pen	push-button pencil	feather	

There is a bar code on each package.
Circle the two bar codes that have same digits.
Then add these digits.

3002101003

3002101004

3082102003

3082102003

3002101103

4002101003

3092102003

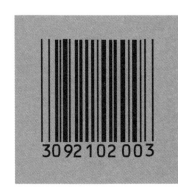

The addition of the digits on the two identical bar codes.

........+ ....+ ....+ ....+ ....+ ....+ ....+ ....+ ....+ ....=........

Connect the first part of a sentence to its matching second part. You will have 4 complete sentences in each box.

• The dog gnaws	the fish.
• The cat eats	on a branch.
• The sparrow is picking	at a bone.
• The monkey stays	some breadcrumbs.

• My sister is going	the journal.
• My father buys	on the blackboard.
• My mother cooks	the meat.
• The teacher is writing	to school.

• I sing	on the door.
• Eric is knocking	an egg.
• The hen lays	a song.
• The doll is sleeping	in the cradle.

• The sun	is up there.
• Robert reads	towards the house.
• The bus runs	soup.
• The cook is cooking	a book.

Write the correct symbol between the two parts of the exercise. You can choose =, < or >.

12 + 8 .... 10 + 9
5 - 4 .... 19 - 18
6 + 5 .... 7 + 4
20 - 9 .... 20 - 10
4 + 5 .... 16 - 4
14 - 11 .... 1 + 1
11 + 3 .... 12 + 4
6 + 6 .... 7 + 3
17 - 8 .... 6 + 3
11 - 4 .... 14 - 7

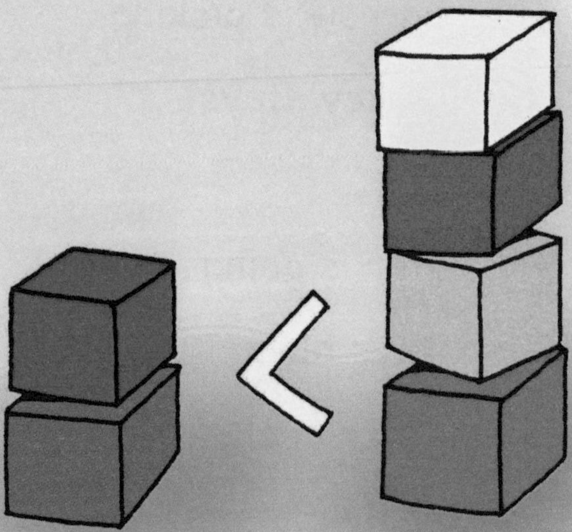

Connect the solution of each problem to a circled number that is smaller than it by one number.

16 - 8 =.......	o	(10)
19 - 17 =.......	o	(7)
15 - 4 =.......	o	(9)
12 - 8 =.......	o	(0)
19 - 9 =.......	o	(2)
14 - 7 =.......	o	(6)
6 - 5 =.......	o	(1)
16 - 13 =.......	o	(12)
20 - 7 =.......	o	(15)
18 - 2 =.......	o	(3)

Can you write the number that is missing next to each branch? The total is given above the tree.

16
12 ....
14 ....
6 ....
8 ....
9 ....
14
.... 10
.... 6
.... 11
.... 7
.... 3
9
4 ....
.... 7
6 ....
.... 1
0 ....
14
12 ....
6 ....
13 ....
10 ....
7 ....
15
.... 5
.... 9
.... 13
.... 15
.... 1

Read these sentences carefully and write each person's name under each picture.

1. Mother comes home. She gives Ann a book.
2. Mark is walking. He reads the journal.
3. Father folds the journal. His name is Stan.
4. He takes the letter. The letter is long. Bob reads the letter.
5. Becky is ill. She stays in bed. She reads a book.
6. The teacher reads. She writes the word tree on the blackboard. The teacher's name is Julie.

....

....

....

tree

....

....

....

Susie wants to take some beads from each necklace. Count all of the beads on the necklace and then take the beads off that are separated at the end of the string. Count the remaining beads and write each subtraction on the dotted lines.

Example:  7 - 2 = 5

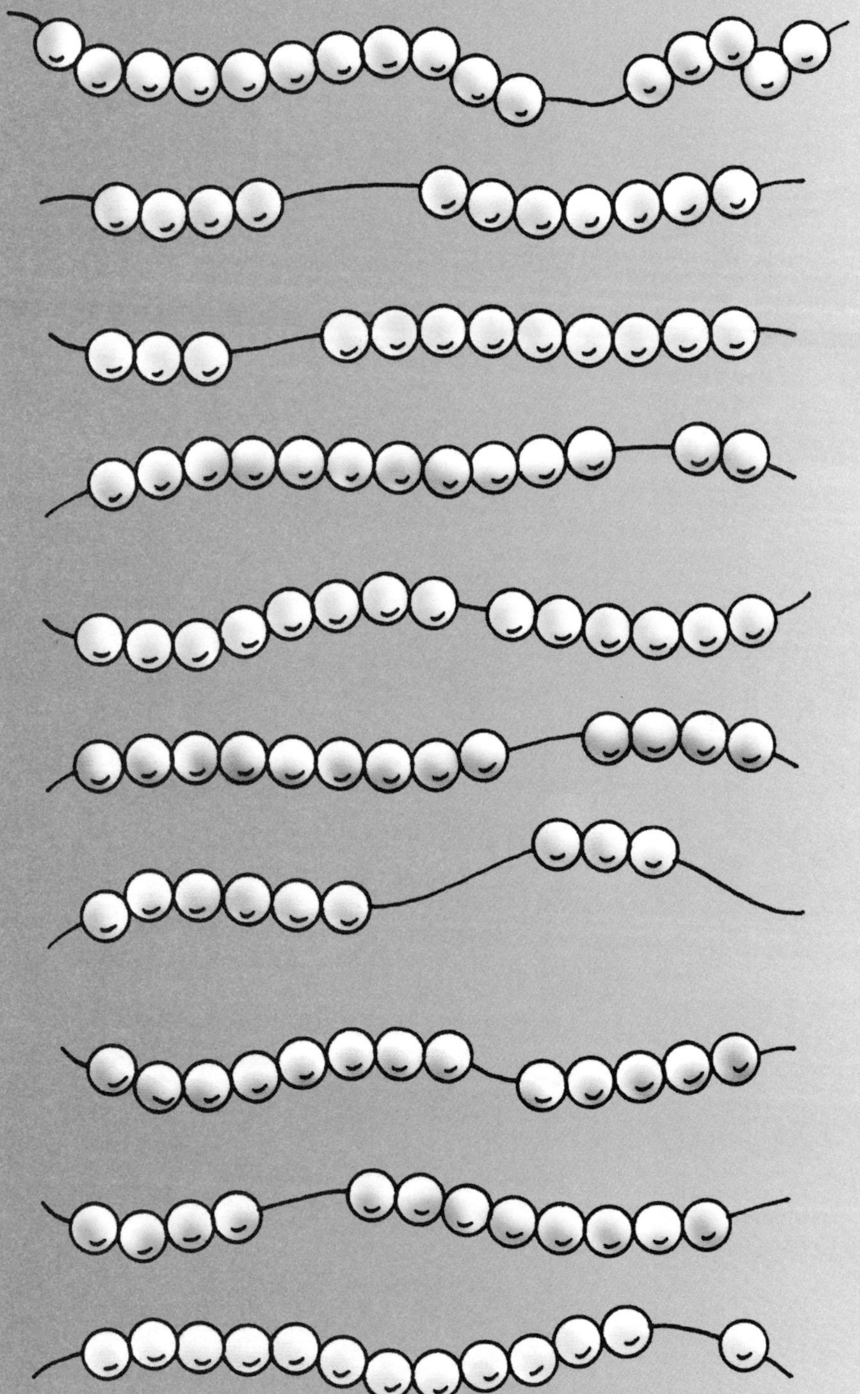

....

....

....

....

....

....

....

....

....

....

Look carefully at each picture and color the street lights as it suits each action.

red

green

Write the correct numbers. The problem must have the same result on the left side of the = sign as on its right side.

5	+	1	=	....	+	3
....	+	3	=	....	+	5
4	-	0	=	....	+	....
....	-	2	=	7	-	4
10	+	....	=	16	-	1
....	+	....	=	....	+	8
9	+	9	=	....	-	2
6	+	....	=	5	+	....
12	-	4	=	....	+	....
....	-	1	=	7	+	10
....	-	....	=	6	+	6
15	-	7	=	9	-	....
7	+	....	=	....	+	....
14	-	....	=	10	+	2
....	+	....	=	....	+	....

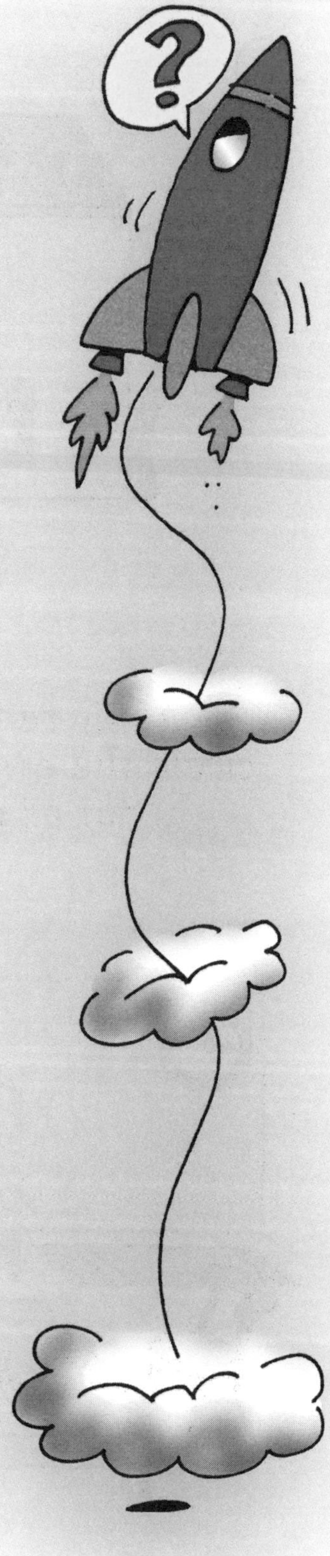
?

Read the following sentences carefully and draw what they tell.

There is a dog cage on the left side of the house.
The house has a door.
There is smoke over the chimney.
The cat sleeps on the roof.
A cloud covers the sun.
There is a bicycle on the right side of the house.

After reading the following sentences, circle the errors in the picture. Pay attention; not all of the sentences are false.

There is a pear on the table.
The closet is closed.
There is a vase on the closet.
It's two o'clock.
The chair is toppled over on the floor.
There is a carpet in front of the closet.

To have a total of 15 in each row, you must throw a card out. Circle the card.

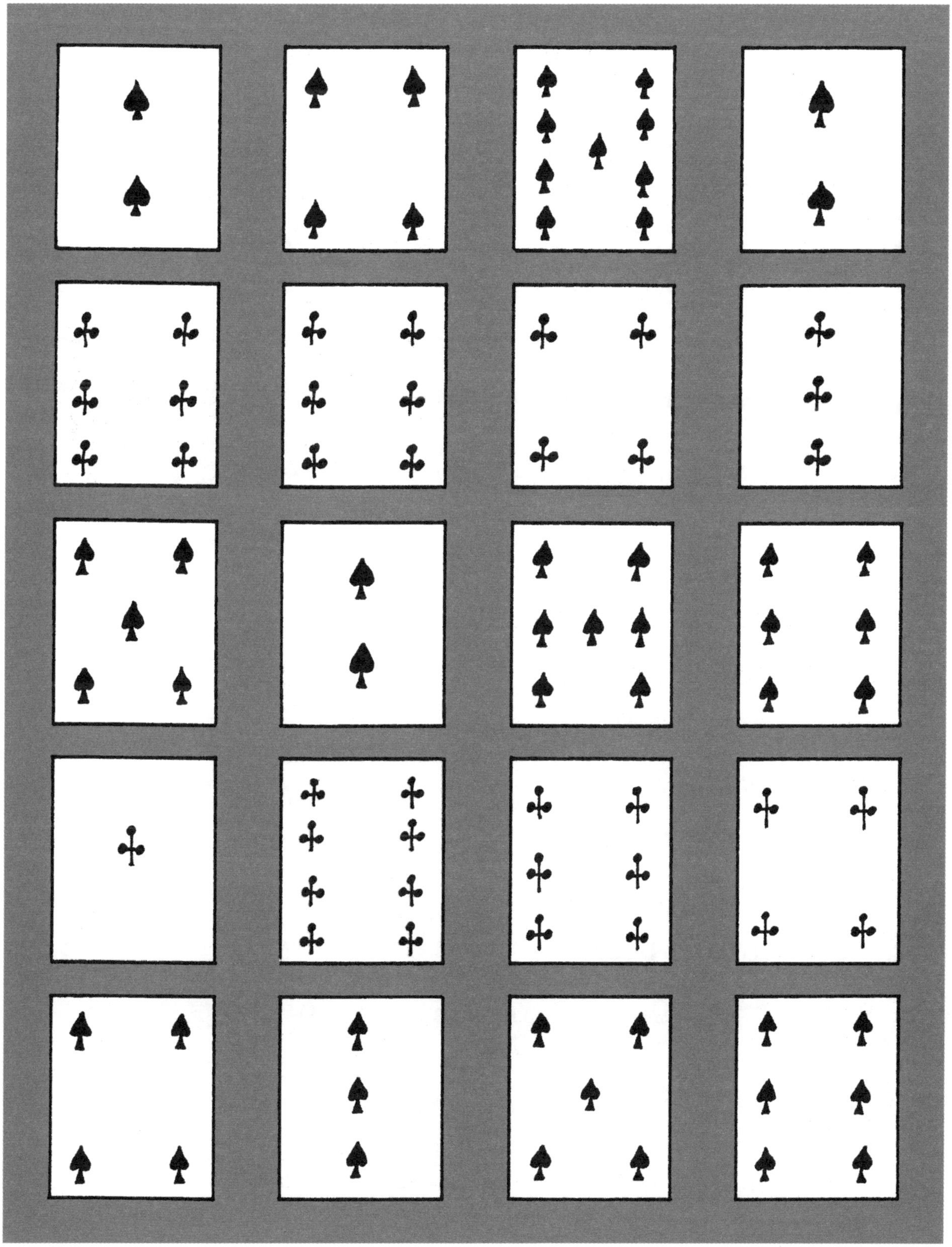

Read the following sentences carefully and write the number of each sentence under the right picture.

....

1. The teacher is at the blackboard.
2. She is wearing a skirt.
3. She is sitting on the seesaw.
4. The sun is shining.
5. Tom is on the seesaw.
6. Tom is reading a book.
7. Eric is eating a pear.
8. Robert is eating a cracker.
9. Bill is looking at the blackboard.
10. Eric is seated on the grass.

Can you connect the dots from 2 to 17 in the right order?
To find these numbers, solve the additions and subtractions.
You must ignore the results 0, 1, 18, 19 and 20.

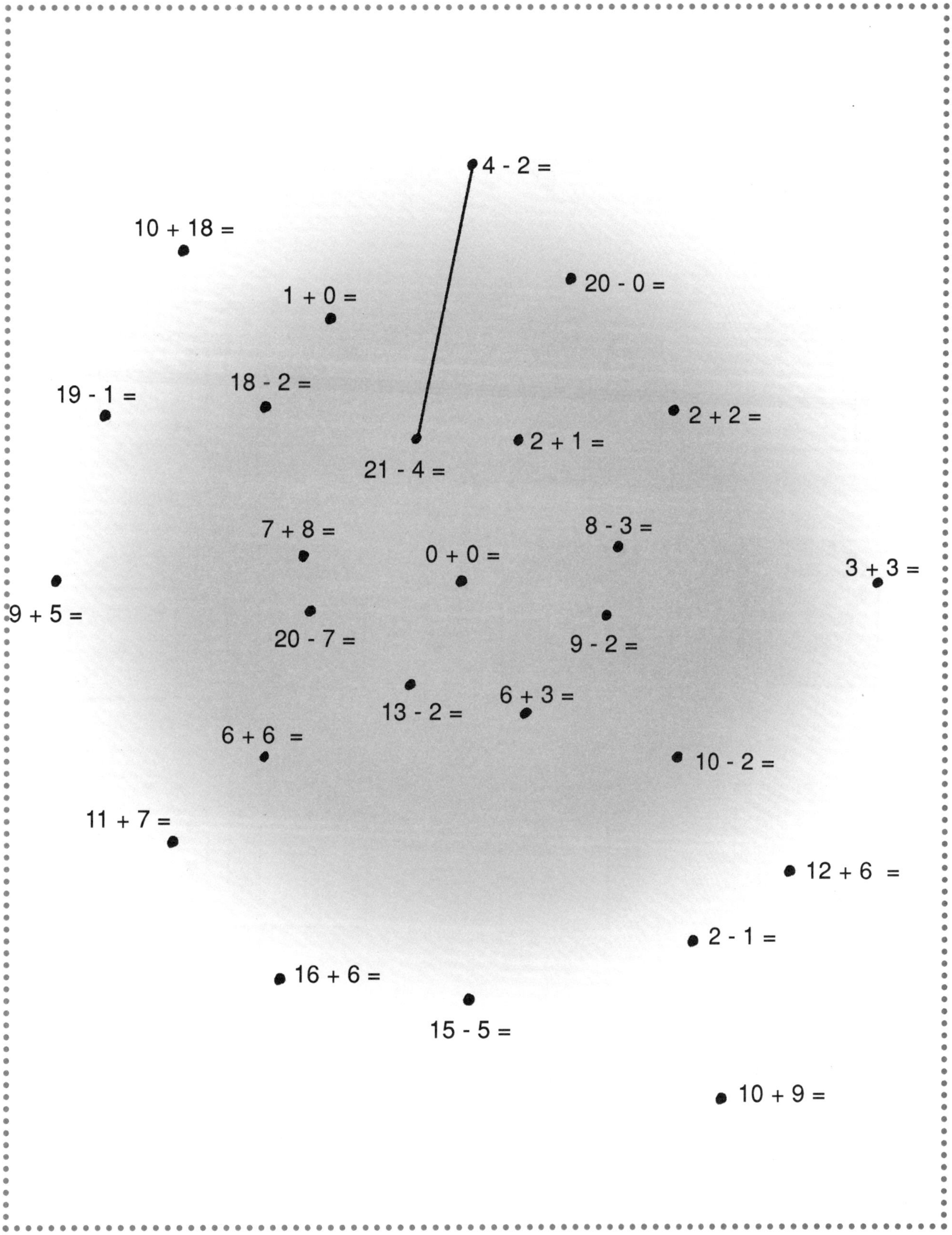
4 - 2 =
10 + 18 =
20 - 0 =
1 + 0 =
19 - 1 =
18 - 2 =
2 + 2 =
2 + 1 =
21 - 4 =
7 + 8 =
8 - 3 =
0 + 0 =
3 + 3 =
9 + 5 =
20 - 7 =
9 - 2 =
6 + 3 =
13 - 2 =
6 + 6 =
10 - 2 =
11 + 7 =
12 + 6 =
2 - 1 =
16 + 6 =
15 - 5 =
10 + 9 =

In the classroom, the pupils have to throw two dice. Write on the bare die in each row the points that are necessary to obtain the same total as on the other two dice on the right side of the page.

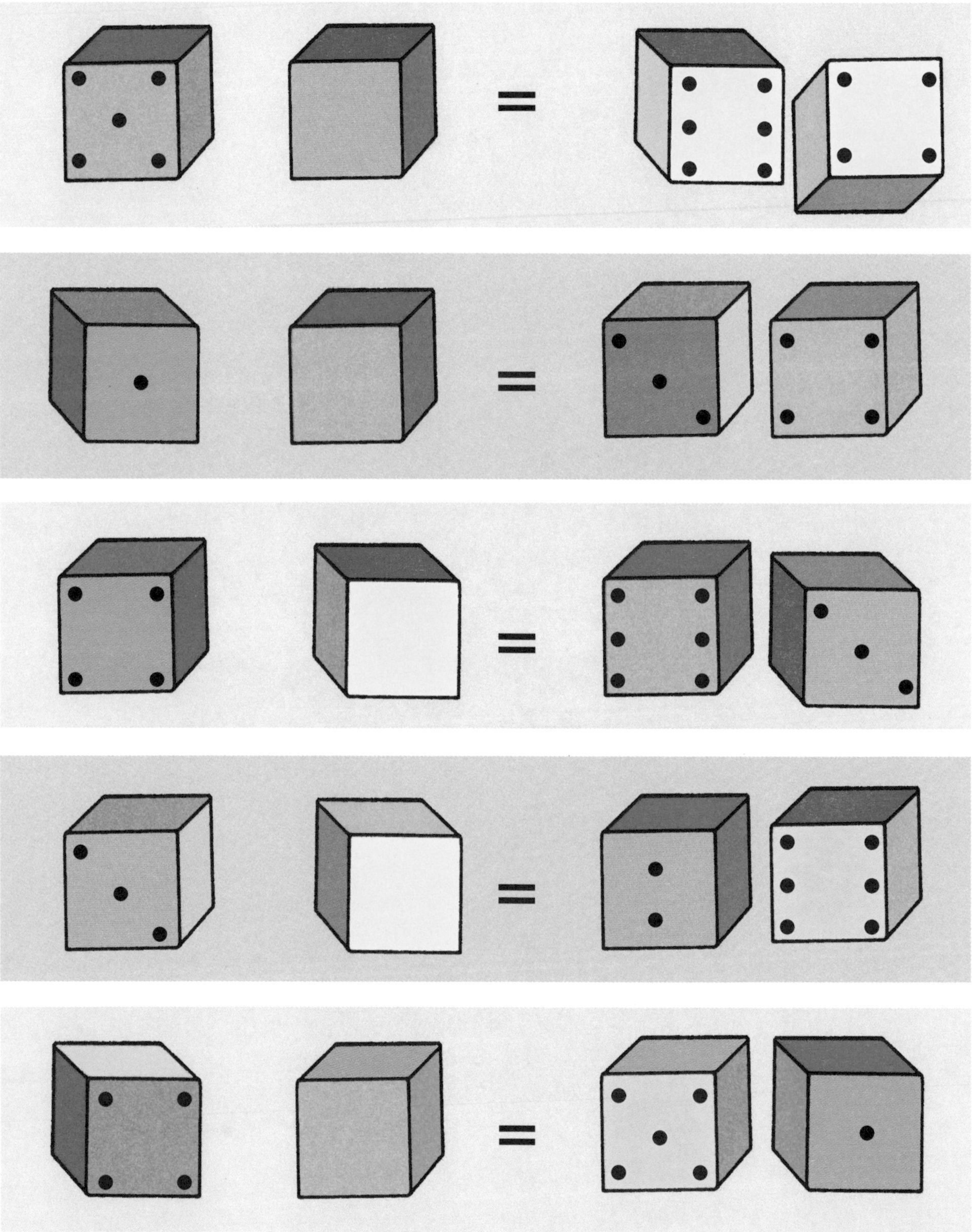

On each row, cross out the object that does not belong there.

fine	fire	flower	for	look
879	678	987	789	897
mmm	nnn	uuu	mmm	nnn
wall	ball	hall	milk	mall
5	8	4	25	7
123	809	345	678	789
db	pq	kt	bd	pq
101	404	333	606	707
w	wx	wxy	vvv	wxyz
222	455	333	888	666

At this party, the children may play various games.
But they must pay for them with little cards.
Each child must save 4 cards for the end of the party,
when they will be able to buy french fries.

For each kid, write how many cards he or she may spend on games. Write the subtraction under the cards.

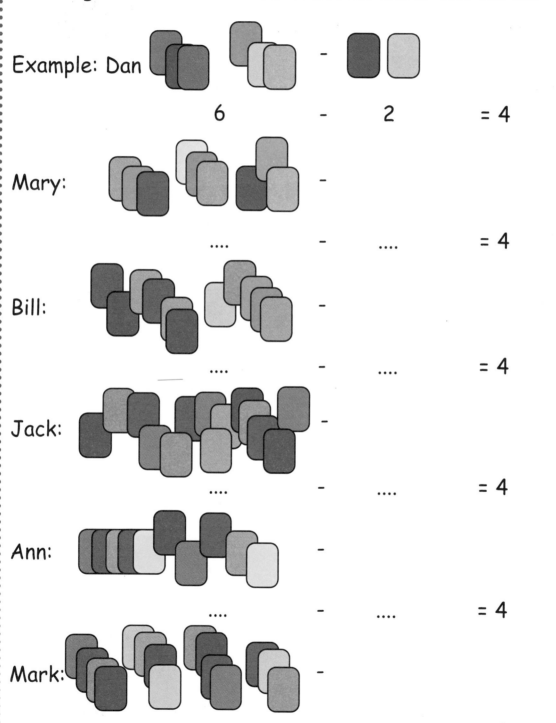

Example: Dan 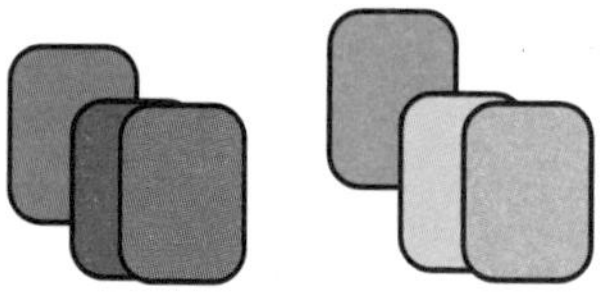 - 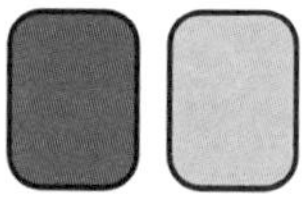

6 - 2 = 4

Mary: 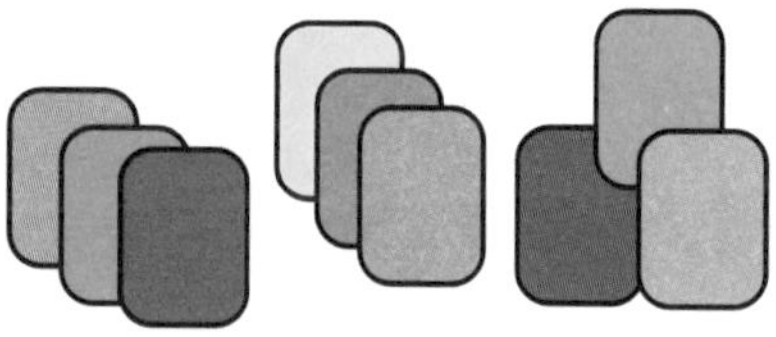 -

.... - .... = 4

Bill: 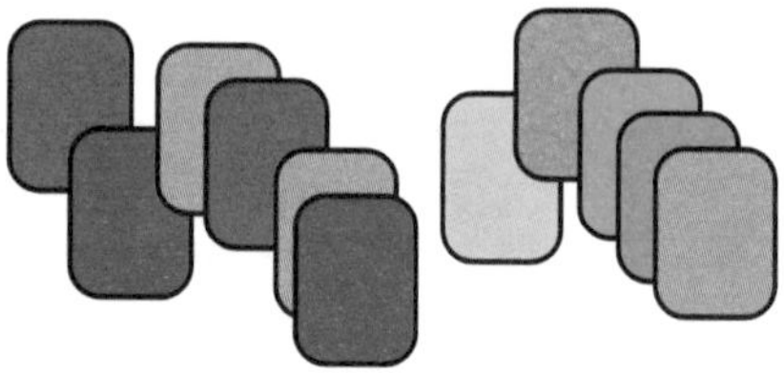 -

.... - .... = 4

Jack: 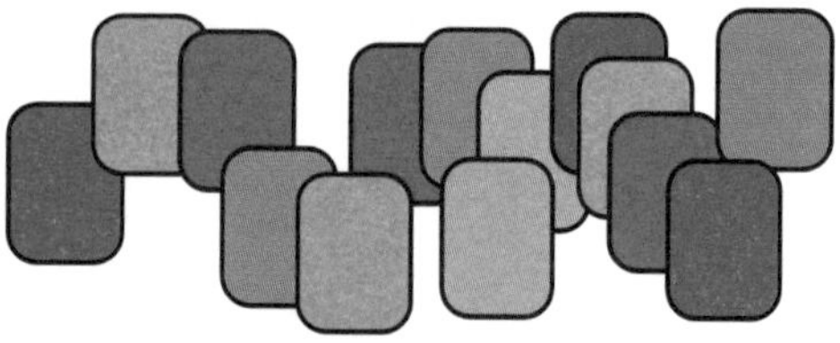 -

.... - .... = 4

Ann: 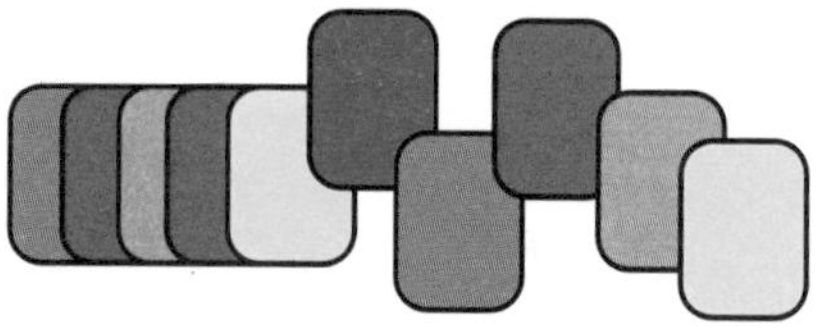 -

.... - .... = 4

Mark: 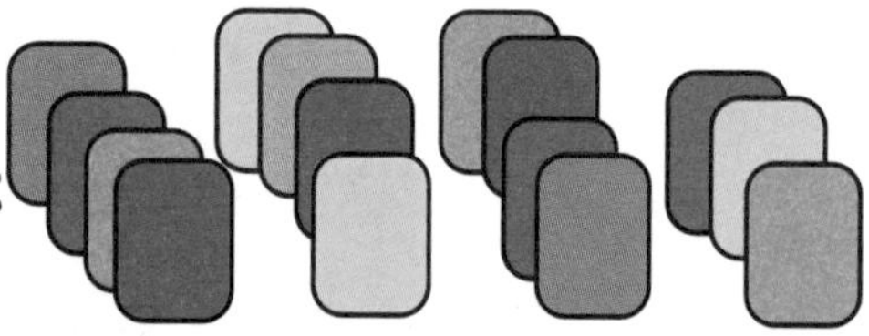 -

.... - .... = 4

Solve the following problems. In each box, the answers of all of the problems must be the same.

15 + ... = 7 + ... = 10 + ... = 11 + ... = 2 + ... = 4 + ... = 17 + ... = 9 + ... = 13 + ... = 6 + ... =	20

...... - 9 = ... - 5 = ... - 10 = ... - 2 = ... - 11 = ... - 4 = ... - 8 = ... - 7 = ... - 1 = ... - 6 =	9

15 + ... = 7 + ... = 10 + ... = 11 + ... = 2 + ... = 4 + ... = 17 + ... = 9 + ... = 13 + ... = 6 + ... =	18

...... - 9 = ... - 5 = ... - 10 = ... - 2 = ... - 11 = ... - 4 = ... - 8 = ... - 7 = ... - 1 = ... - 6 =	6

Some sports can be played in the winter and some others in the summer. Write next to each shadow the initial of the season in which it is played.
W = winter   S = summer.

In a dart game, all of the children want to have 20 points. Color those rings of the target that each child must hit to obtain 20 points. Each child may shoot two times.

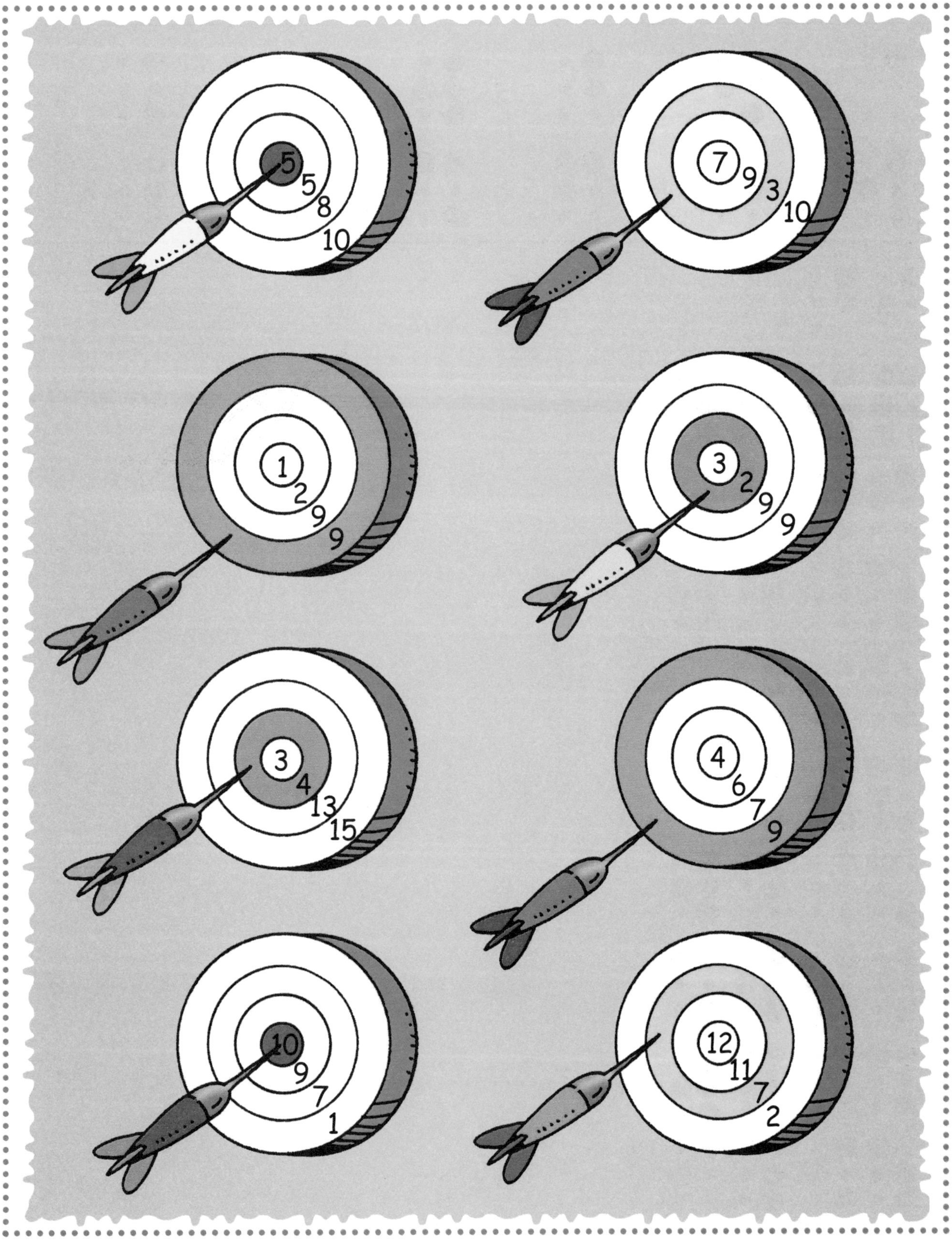
5
5
8
10
7
9
3
10
1
2
9
9
3
2
9
9
3
4
13
15
4
6
7
9
10
9
7
1
12
11
7
2

Paul's friend is blind and is learning to read with his fingers. Help Paul write what his friend can already read in the Braille alphabet.

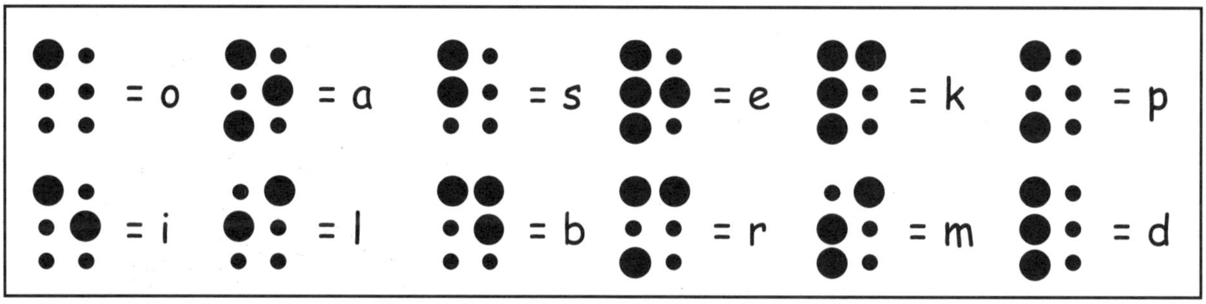
= o
= a
= s
= e
= k
= p
= i
= l
= b
= r
= m
= d

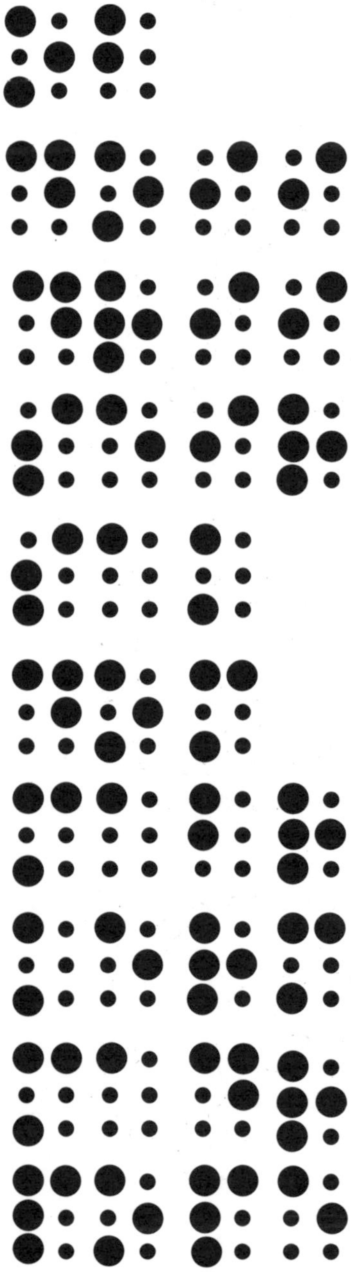

= ....

= ....

= ....

= ....

= ....

= ....

= ....

= ....

= ....

= ....

Help the teacher correct her pupils' homework. Cross out the mistakes, write the correct answer next to each problem, and give marks for each pupil.

Nick: ....../10

10 + 5	=	15	......
6 + 6	=	13	......
7 + 8	=	16	......
4 + 4	=	8	......
11 + 9	=	18	......
13 + 6	=	19	......
9 + 8	=	17	......
4 + 12	=	16	......
5 + 13	=	20	......
17 + 2	=	19	......

Eric: ....../10

20 - 9	=	11	......
11 - 8	=	3	......
8 - 7	=	0	......
18 - 9	=	8	......
14 - 5	=	9	......
16 - 12	=	1	......
9 - 2	=	4	......
13 - 11	=	2	......
15 - 8	=	7	......
20 - 10	=	10	......

Jack: ....../10

6 + 7	=	14	......
12 + 8	=	20	......
3 + 4	=	7	......
8 + 7	=	15	......
11 + 6	=	15	......
14 + 3	=	17	......
15 + 4	=	20	......
1 + 15	=	16	......
17 + 3	=	19	......
9 + 9	=	17	......

Mary: ....../10

13 - 7	=	6	......
15 - 11	=	4	......
12 - 8	=	4	......
5 - 2	=	3	......
16 - 14	=	1	......
18 - 3	=	15	......
7 - 7	=	1	......
14 - 13	=	1	......
20 - 7	=	13	......
19 - 5	=	14	......

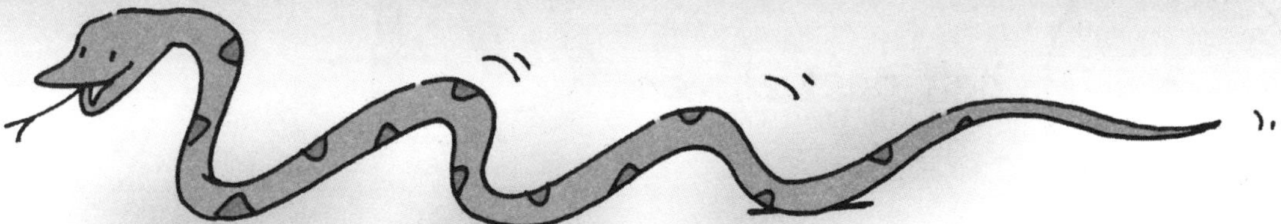

For each clock in the left column, draw the hands at their proper places. Then for each clock in the right column, turn the hands back half an hour.

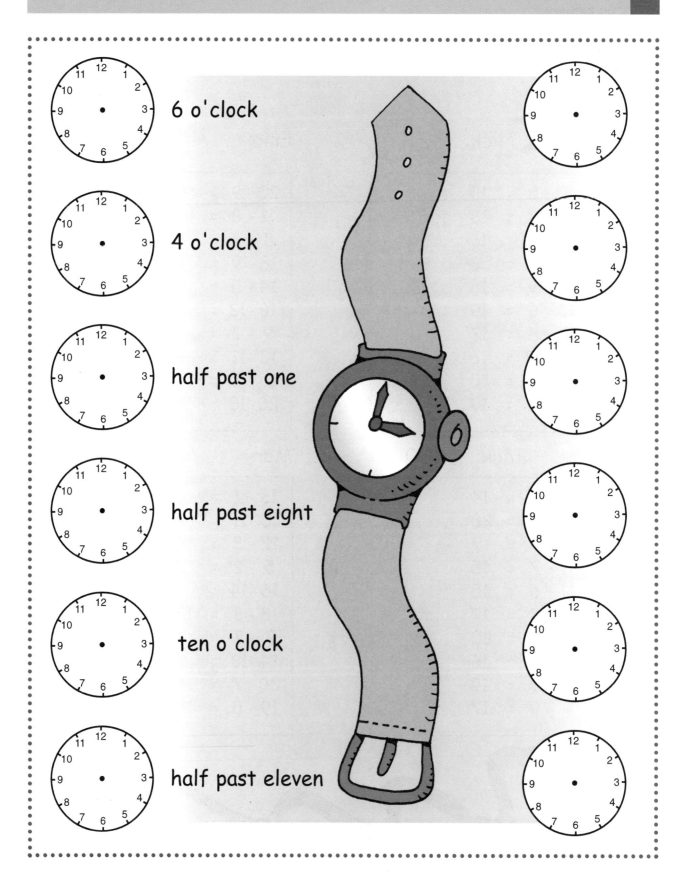

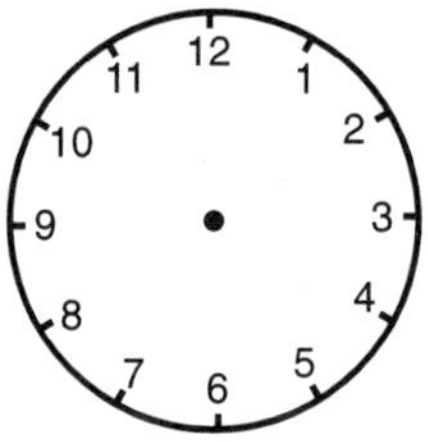
6 o'clock
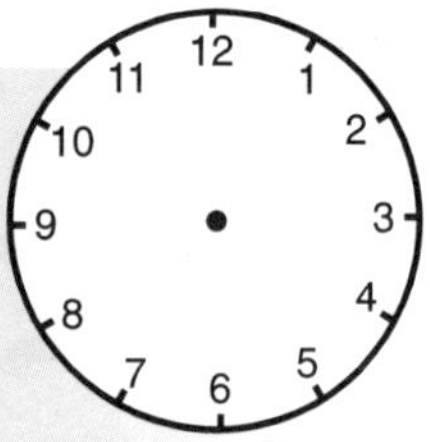

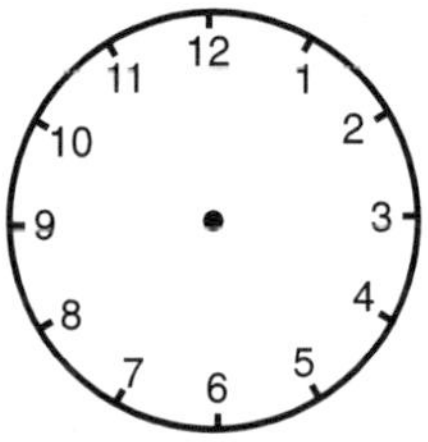
4 o'clock
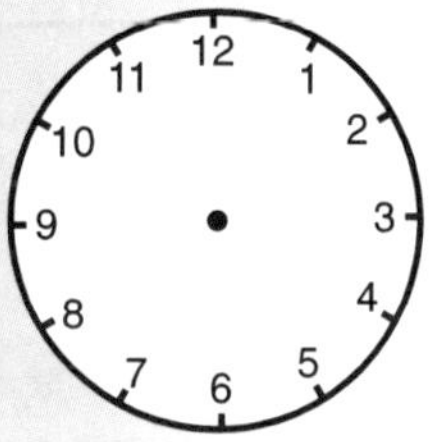

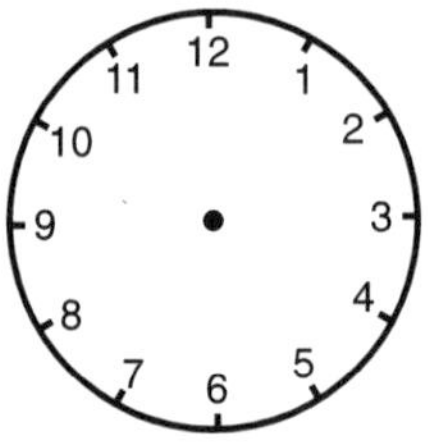
half past one
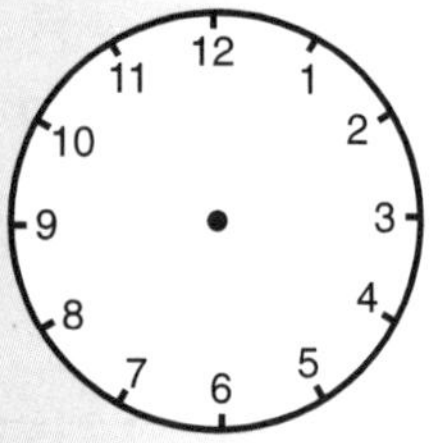

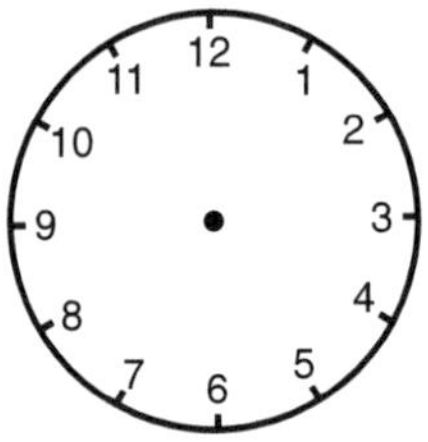
half past eight
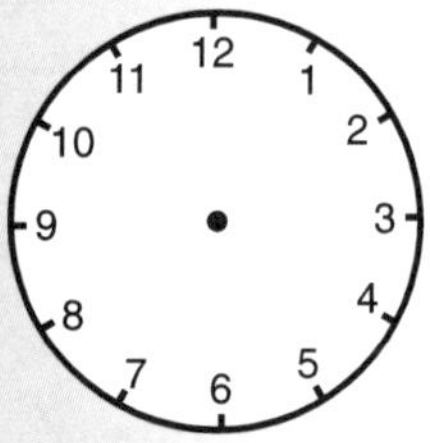

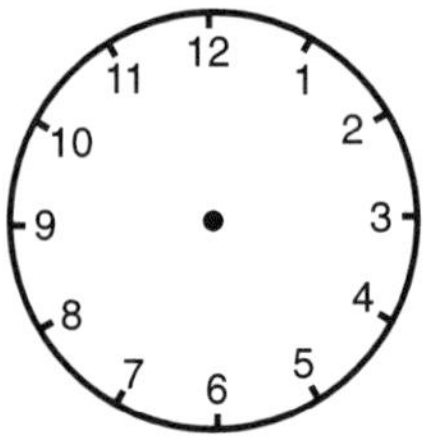
ten o'clock
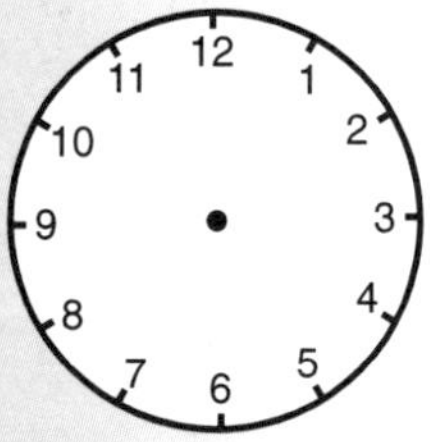

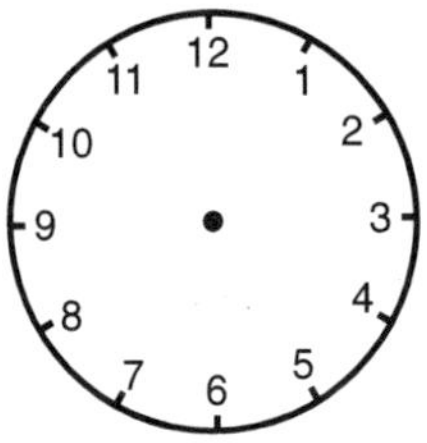
half past eleven
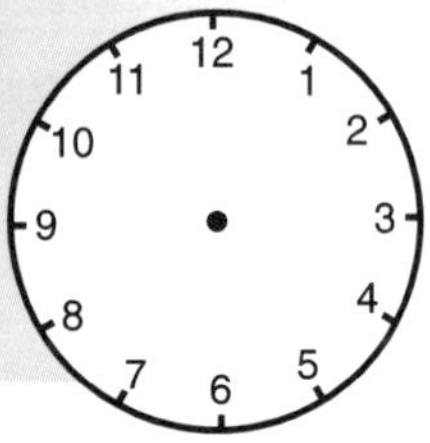

Read the sentences at the bottom of the page carefully and cross out the rows and columns that have to be eliminated. You will then discover the object I am looking for.

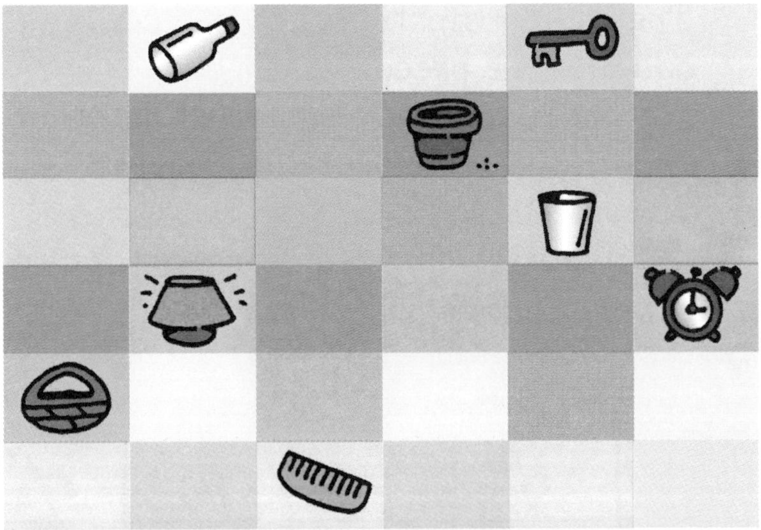

1. I am somewhere on the left side of the clock.
2. I am on a row below the bottle.
3. I am somewhere on the right side of the basket.
4. I am somewhere above the lamp.
5. I am on a row above the glass.
6. I am somewhere on the right side of the comb.
7. I am on the left side of the key.
8. I AM A...

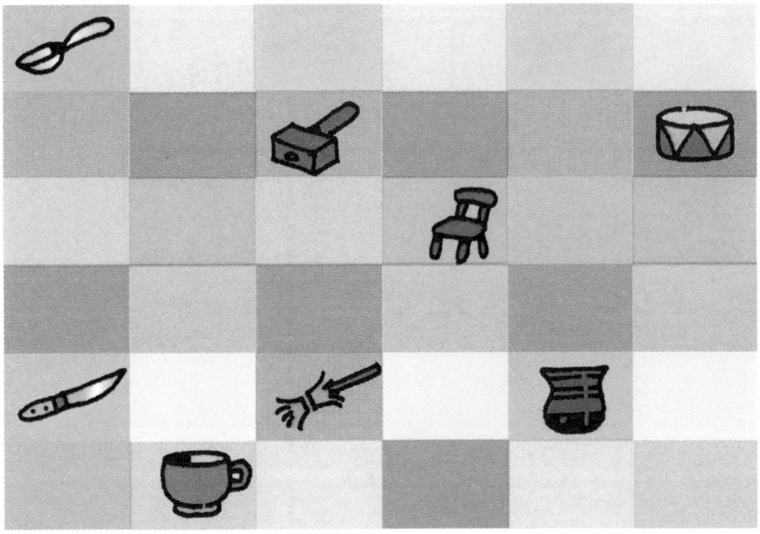

1. Am over 2 boxes away from the drum.
2. I am somewhere below the spoon.
3. I am somewhere on the right side of the knife.
4. I am over 2 boxes away from the chair.
5. I am somewhere on the left side of the vase.
6. I am below the broom.
7. I AM A...

The captain and the pirate each want to be the first one to get to the treasure, but they must take different ways. Mark their ways by crossing out the boxes. The boxes crossed out must be adjoining.

The captain starts from 0 and each time he must add 3 to the preceding number. The pirate starts from 20 and each time must subtract 4 from the preceding number.

For which one of them did you cross out fewer boxes?

It is the..

0	4	9	17	19
2	3	11	15	20
6	10	12	14	16
9	8	13	12	11
11	12	16	9	8
10	7	15	19	4
9	6	20	18	0

Fill in each box with the missing number.
Solve the problem starting from the number that is written in the left box and continue by building on the preceding solution.

......	
	+6
......	
	+5
......	
	+4
......	
	+3
2	

19	
	-4
......	
	-3
......	
	-4
......	
	-3
......	

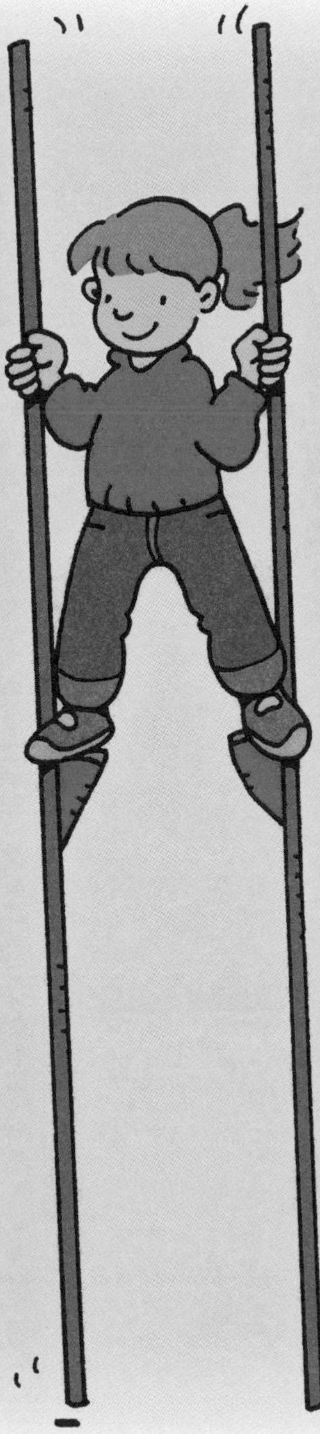

......	
	+5
......	
	+4
......	
	+3
......	
	+2
5	

17	
	-9
......	
	-2
......	
	-5
......	
	-1
......	

Solve the following subtractions. Then count the identical solutions and write the result in the frame, where indicated.

19 - 13 = ...

16 - 11 = ...

18 - 15 = ...

12 - 8 = ...

20 - 14 = ...

9 - 7 = ...

11 - 8 = ...

14 - 12 = ...

19 - 16 = ...

8 - 5 = ...

19 - 15 = ...

7 - 4 = ...

20 - 15 = ...

15 - 13 = ...

8 - 3 = ...

16 - 12 = ...

4 - 2 = ...

10 - 5 = ...

11 - 6 = ...

17 - 14 = ...

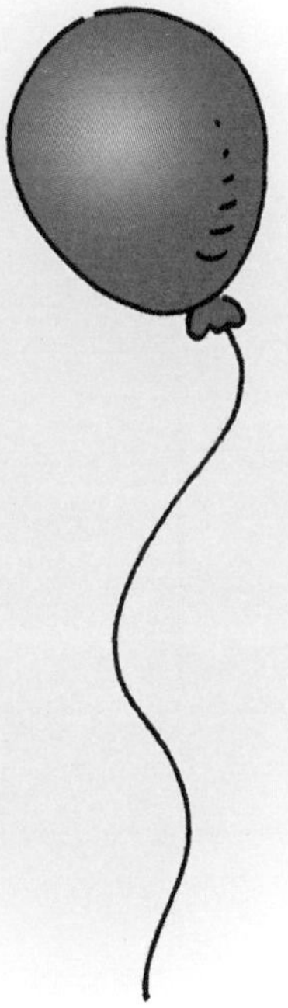

2 identical numbers = ...
3 identical numbers = ...
4 identical numbers = ...
5 identical numbers = ...
6 identical numbers = ...

+ 20

page 3

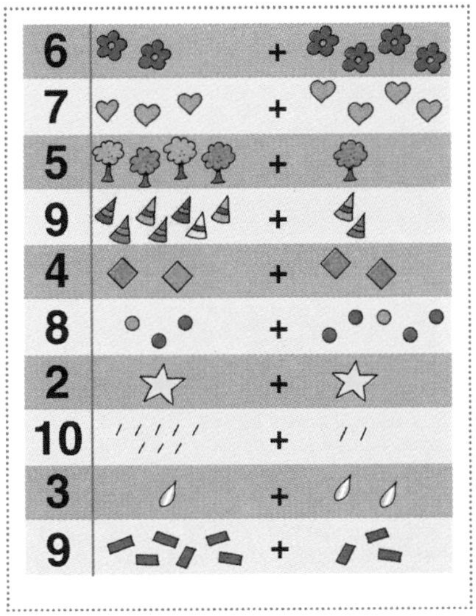
6 +
7 +
5 +
9 +
4 +
8 +
2 +
10 +
3 +
9 +

page 4

SUMMER
WINTER
SPRING
AUTUMN

page 5

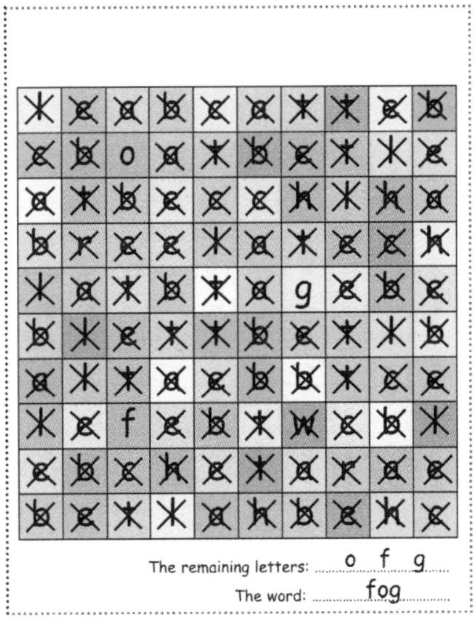
o
g
f
The remaining letters: o f g
The word: fog

page 6

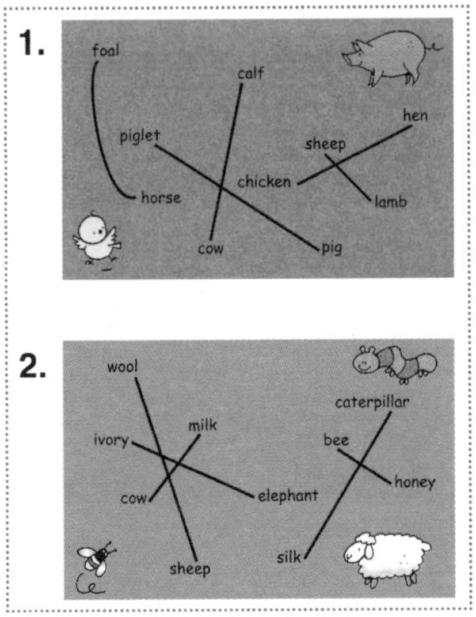
1.
foal
calf
hen
piglet
sheep
chicken
horse
lamb
cow
pig
2.
wool
caterpillar
milk
ivory
bee
honey
cow
elephant
silk
sheep

page 7

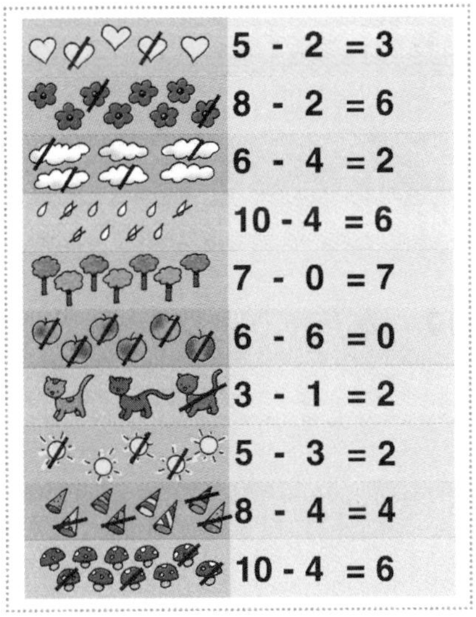
5 - 2 = 3
8 - 2 = 6
6 - 4 = 2
10 - 4 = 6
7 - 0 = 7
6 - 6 = 0
3 - 1 = 2
5 - 3 = 2
8 - 4 = 4
10 - 4 = 6

page 8

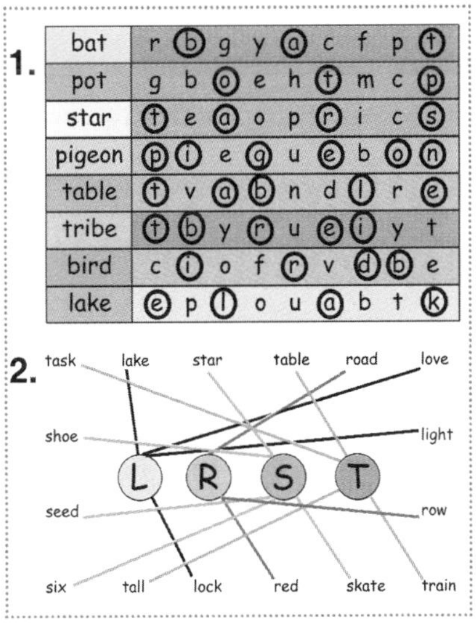
1.
bat r b g y a c f p t
pot g b o e h t m c p
star t e a o p r i c s
pigeon p i e g u e b o n
table t v a b n d l r e
tribe t b y r u e i y t
bird c i o f r v d b e
lake e p l o u a b t k
2.
task
lake
star
table
road
love
shoe
light
L
R
S
T
seed
row
six
tall
lock
red
skate
train

page 9

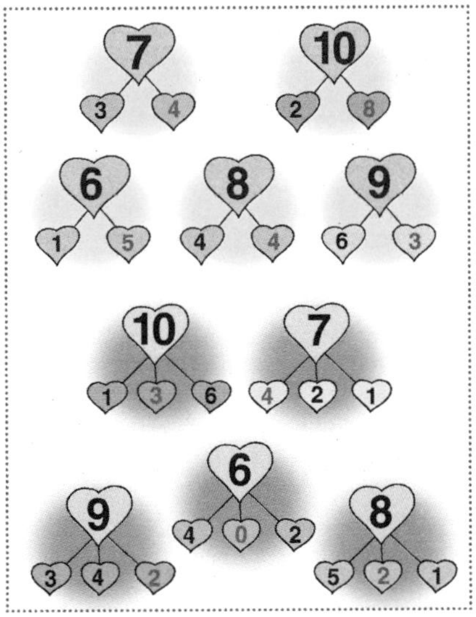
7
3
4
10
2
8
6
1
5
8
4
4
9
6
3
10
1
3
6
7
4
2
1
6
4
0
2
9
3
4
2
8
5
2
1

page 10

2 2 2
8 8 8
0 0 0
9 9 9
5 5 5
1 1 1

page 11

There is a tree.
The pigeon is old.
I am Paul.
The house is small.
Fluffy is the cat.
The cat loves meat.
The cat is in the tree.
Jack lives in the house.

page 12

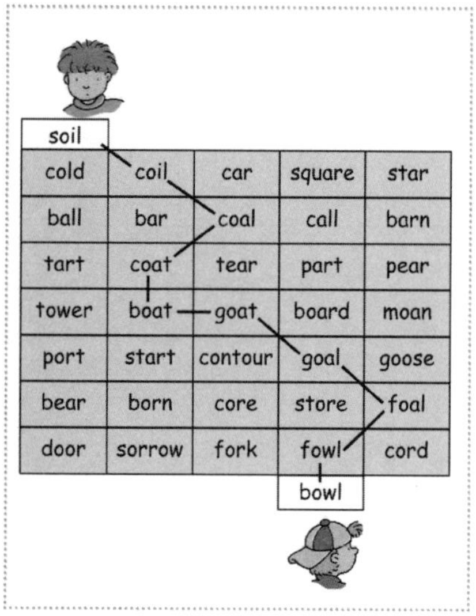
soil
cold coil car square star
ball bar coal call barn
tart coat tear part pear
tower boat goat board moan
port start contour goal goose
bear born core store foal
door sorrow fork fowl cord
bowl

page 13

cow
fish
mouse
cat
bird
mole
dog
snail
shark

page 14

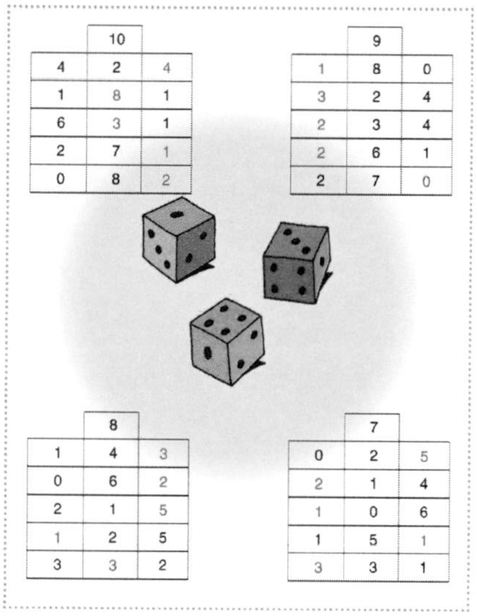
10
4 2 4
1 8 1
6 3 1
2 7 1
0 8 2
9
1 8 0
3 2 4
2 3 4
2 6 1
2 7 0
8
1 4 3
0 6 2
2 1 5
1 2 5
3 3 2
7
0 2 5
2 1 4
1 0 6
1 5 1
3 3 1

page 15

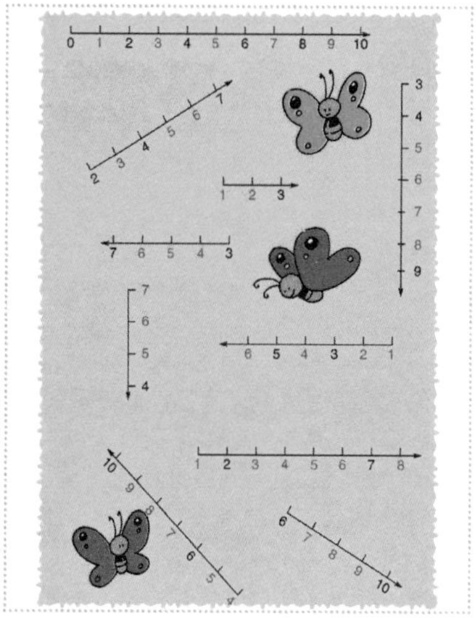

page 16

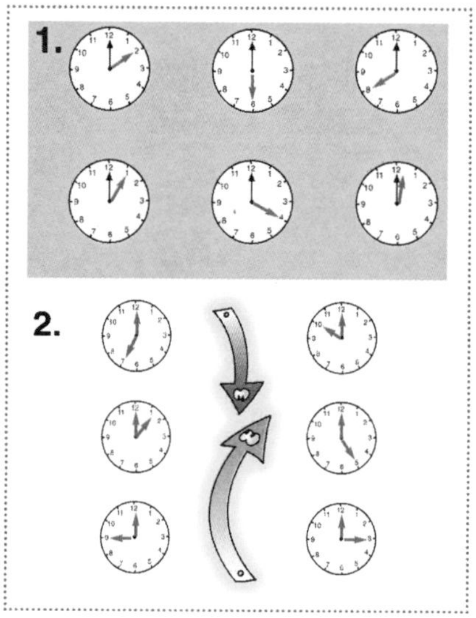
1.
2.

page 17

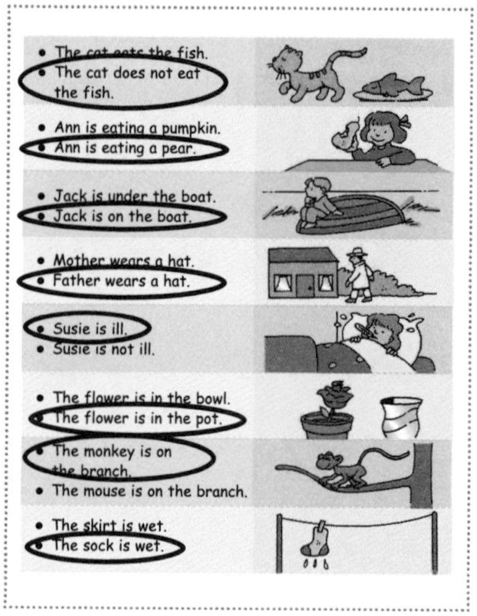
The cat eats the fish.
The cat does not eat the fish.
Ann is eating a pumpkin.
Ann is eating a pear.
Jack is under the boat.
Jack is on the boat.
Mother wears a hat.
Father wears a hat.
Susie is ill.
Susie is not ill.
The flower is in the bowl.
The flower is in the pot.
The monkey is on the branch.
The mouse is on the branch.
The skirt is wet.
The sock is wet.

page 18

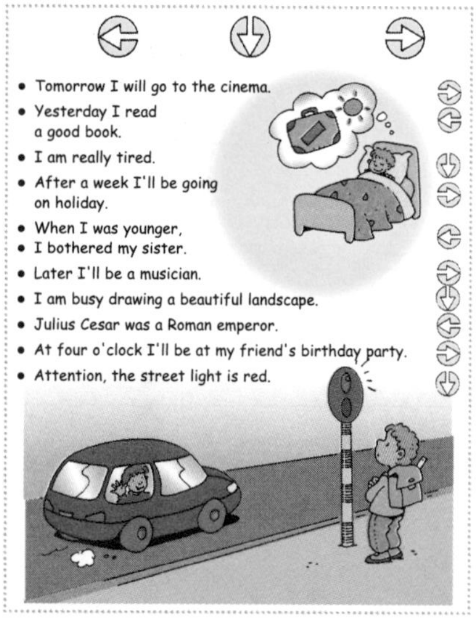
Tomorrow I will go to the cinema.
Yesterday I read a good book.
I am really tired.
After a week I'll be going on holiday.
When I was younger,
I bothered my sister.
Later I'll be a musician.
I am busy drawing a beautiful landscape.
Julius Cesar was a Roman emperor.
At four o'clock I'll be at my friend's birthday party.
Attention, the street light is red.

page 19

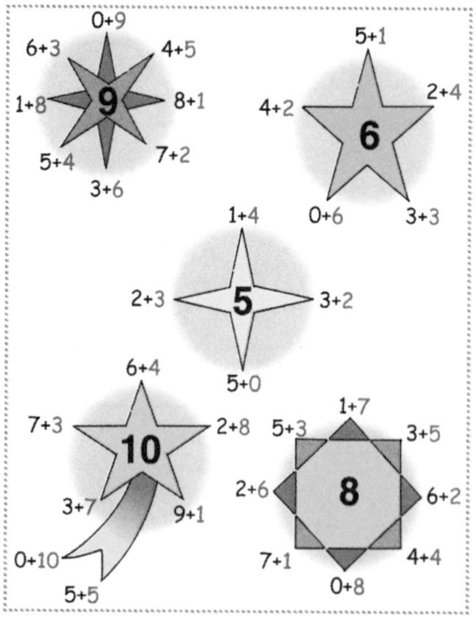
9
0+9 4+5 8+1 7+2 3+6 5+4 1+8 6+3
6
5+1 2+4 3+3 0+6 4+2
5
1+4 3+2 5+0 2+3
10
6+4 2+8 9+1 5+5 0+10 3+7 7+3
8
1+7 3+5 6+2 4+4 0+8 7+1 2+6 5+3

page 20

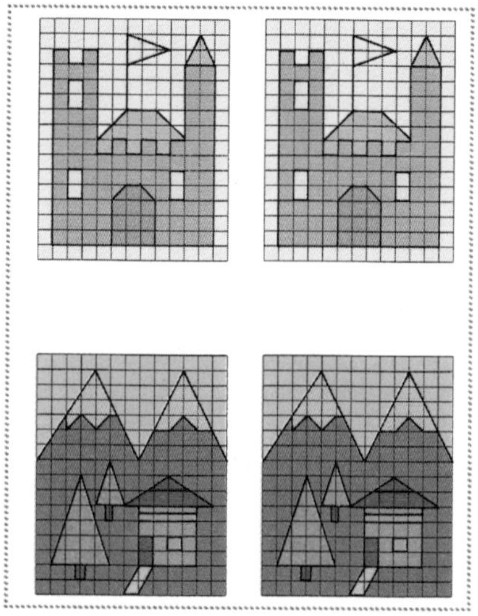

page 21

Tim
Flipper
Fluffy
Cheeta
Sophia
Spike
Billy
Kaa

page 22

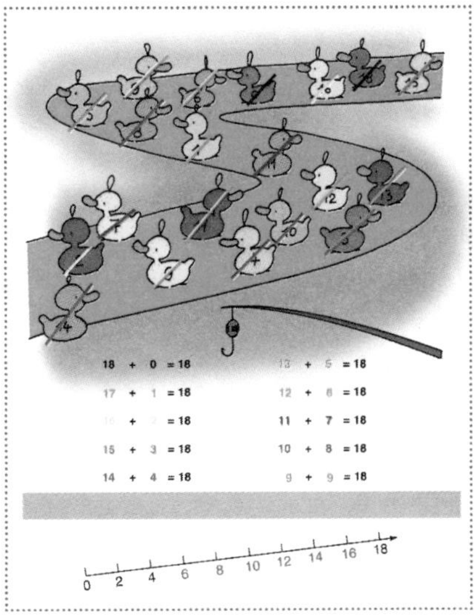

18 + 0 = 18
17 + 1 = 18
15 + 3 = 18
14 + 4 = 18
12 + 6 = 18
11 + 7 = 18
10 + 8 = 18
9 + 9 = 18

page 23

page 24

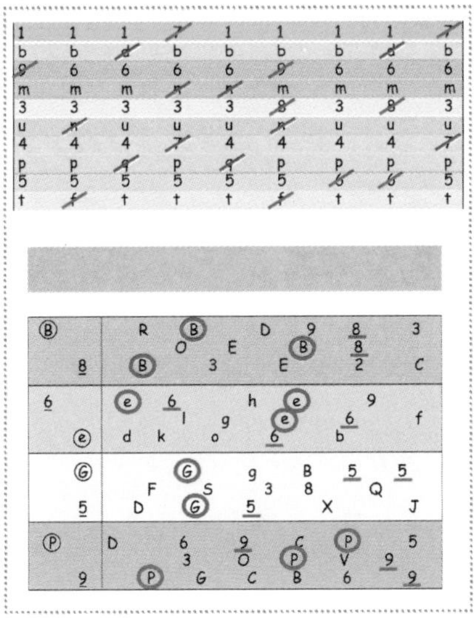

page 25

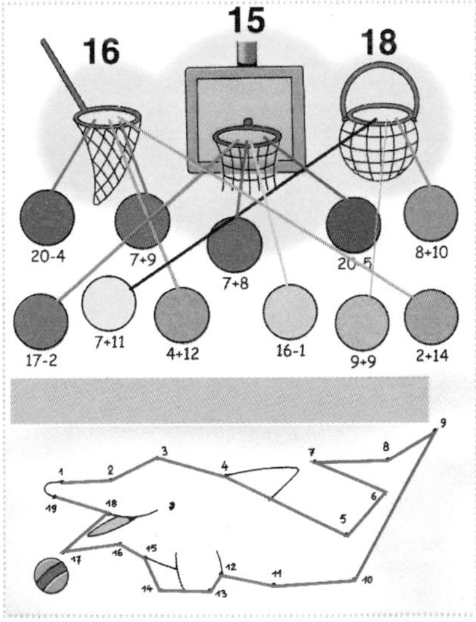

16
15
18
20-4
7+9
7+8
20-5
8+10
17-2
7+11
4+12
16-1
9+9
2+14

page 26

1. The sun is cold.
hot
2. The cat eats fish.
3. I read a plate.
book
4. Father is going to the forest.
5. The cow lays an egg.
hen
6. The moon is red.
silver
7. I hear the ringing bell.
8. I play in the garden.
9. I fly in the sea.
swim
10. Mother is throwing the closet.
cleaning

page 27

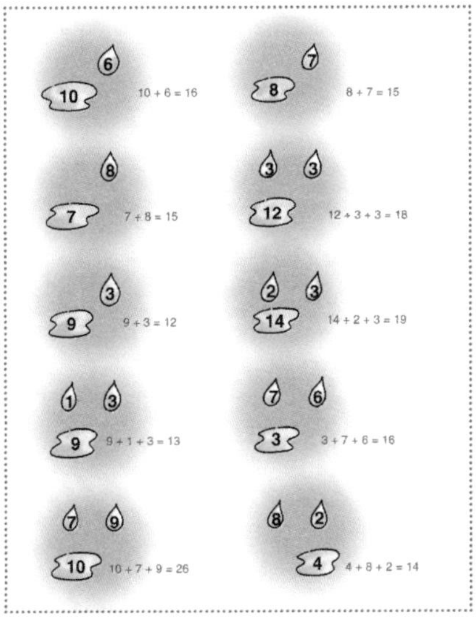

10 + 6 = 16
8 + 7 = 15
7 + 8 = 15
12 + 3 + 3 = 18
9 + 3 = 12
14 + 2 + 3 = 19
9 + 1 + 3 = 13
3 + 7 + 6 = 16
10 + 7 + 9 = 26
4 + 8 + 2 = 14

page 28

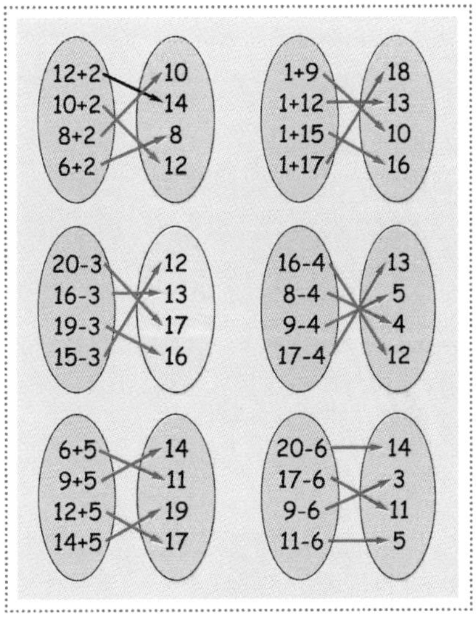

12+2
10+2
8+2
6+2
1+9
1+12
1+15
1+17
20-3
16-3
19-3
15-3
16-4
8-4
9-4
17-4
6+5
9+5
12+5
14+5
20-6
17-6
9-6
11-6

page 29

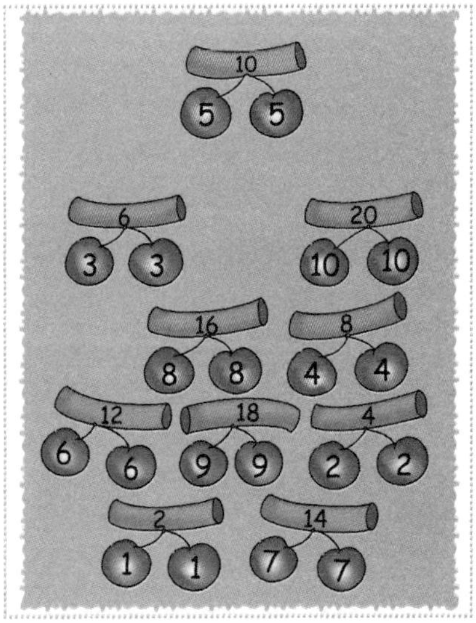

page 30

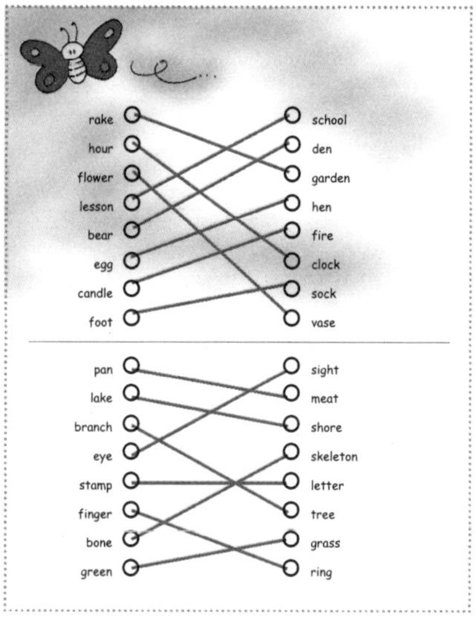

rake
hour
flower
lesson
bear
egg
candle
foot
school
den
garden
hen
fire
clock
sock
vase
pan
lake
branch
eye
stamp
finger
bone
green
sight
meat
shore
skeleton
letter
tree
grass
ring

page 31

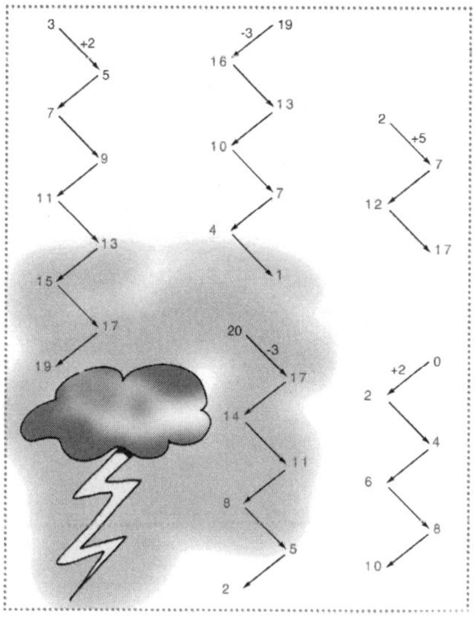

3 +2 5 7 9 11 13 15 17 19
19 -3 16 13 10 7 4 1
2 +5 7 12 17
20 -3 17 14 11 8 5 2
0 +2 2 4 6 8 10

page 32

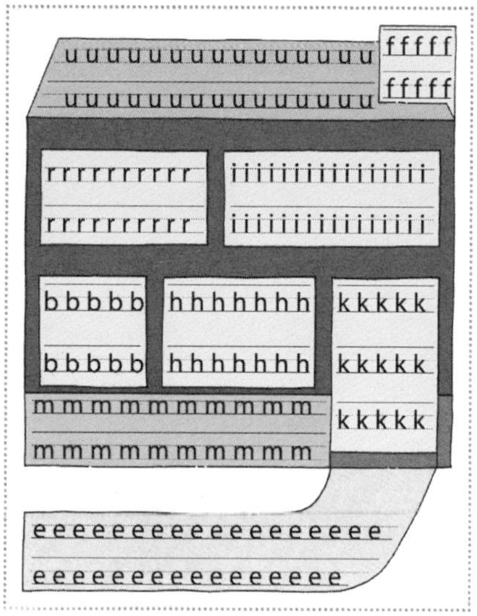

uuuuuuuuuuuuuuu
uuuuuuuuuuuuuuu
fffff
fffff
rrrrrrrrrr
rrrrrrrrrr
iiiiiiiiiiiiiii
iiiiiiiiiiiiiii
bbbbb
bbbbb
hhhhhhh
hhhhhhh
kkkkk
kkkkk
kkkkk
mmmmmmmmmmm
mmmmmmmmmmm
eeeeeeeeeeeeeeeeee
eeeeeeeeeeeeeeee

page 33

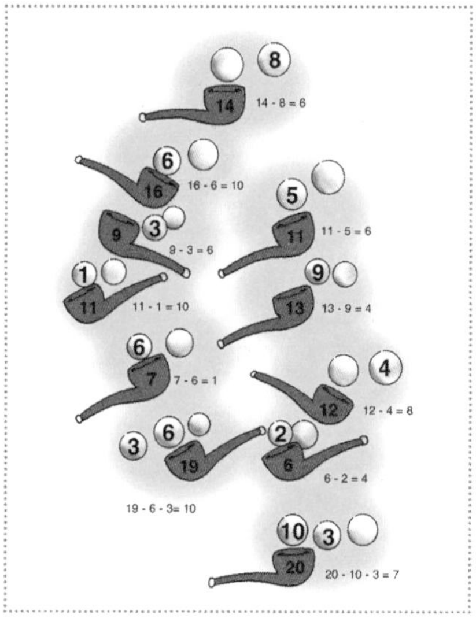

14 - 8 = 6
16 - 6 = 10
9 - 3 = 6
11 - 5 = 6
11 - 1 = 10
13 - 9 = 4
7 - 6 = 1
12 - 4 = 8
6 - 2 = 4
19 - 6 - 3= 10
20 - 10 - 3 = 7

page 34

7
8:30
10:00
12:00
15:30

page 35

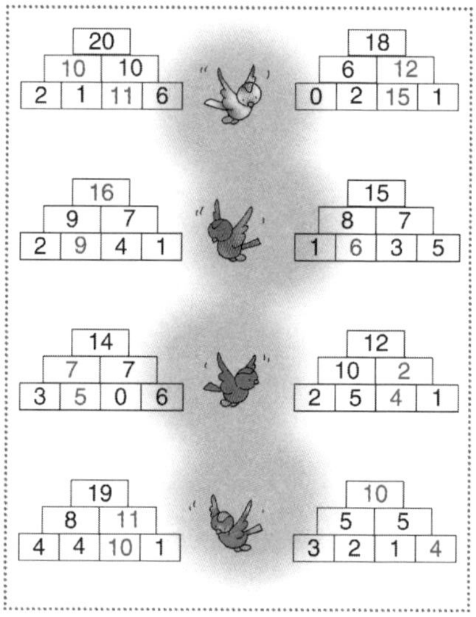

20
10 10
2 1 11 6
18
6 12
0 2 15 1
16
9 7
2 9 4 1
15
8 7
1 6 3 5
14
7 7
3 5 0 6
12
10 2
2 5 4 1
19
8 11
4 4 10 1
10
5 5
3 2 1 4

page 36

18 2
9 11
16 3
7 6
9 10 1
10 10
8 12
15 5
4 10 2
4 16

page 37

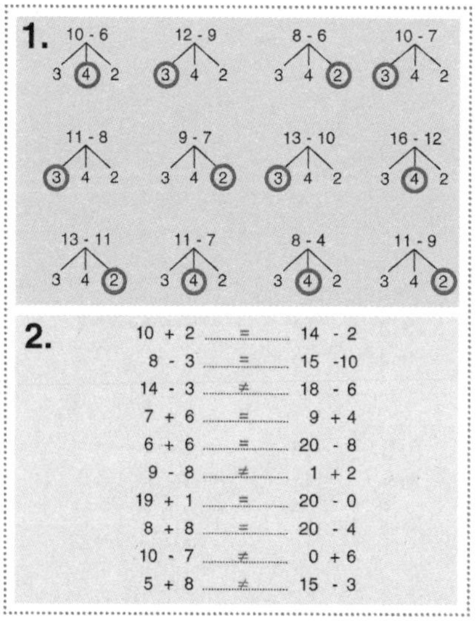

1.
10 - 6
3 4 2
12 - 9
3 4 2
8 - 6
3 4 2
10 - 7
3 4 2
11 - 8
3 4 2
9 - 7
3 4 2
13 - 10
3 4 2
16 - 12
3 4 2
13 - 11
3 4 2
11 - 7
3 4 2
8 - 4
3 4 2
11 - 9
3 4 2
2.
10 + 2 = 14 - 2
8 - 3 = 15 -10
14 - 3 ≠ 18 - 6
7 + 6 = 9 + 4
6 + 6 = 20 - 8
9 - 8 ≠ 1 + 2
19 + 1 = 20 - 0
8 + 8 = 20 - 4
10 - 7 ≠ 0 + 6
5 + 8 ≠ 15 - 3

page 38

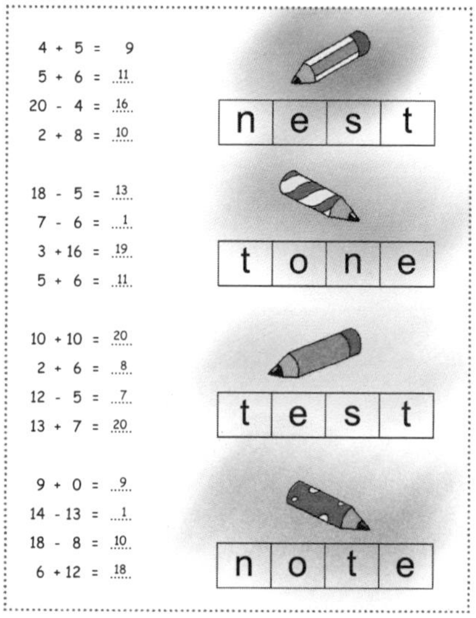

4 + 5 = 9
5 + 6 = 11
20 - 4 = 16
2 + 8 = 10
18 - 5 = 13
7 - 6 = 1
3 + 16 = 19
5 + 6 = 11
10 + 10 = 20
2 + 6 = 8
12 - 5 = 7
13 + 7 = 20
9 + 0 = 9
14 - 13 = 1
18 - 8 = 10
6 + 12 = 18
n e s t
t o n e
t e s t
n o t e

page 39

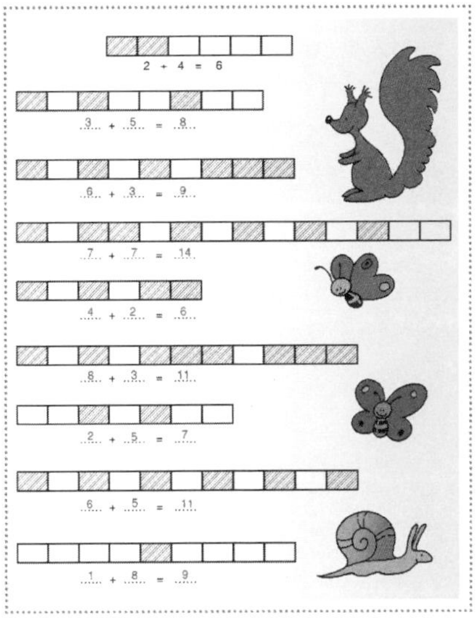
2 + 4 = 6
3 + 5 = 8
6 + 3 = 9
7 + 7 = 14
4 + 2 = 6
8 + 3 = 11
2 + 5 = 7
6 + 5 = 11
1 + 8 = 9

page 40

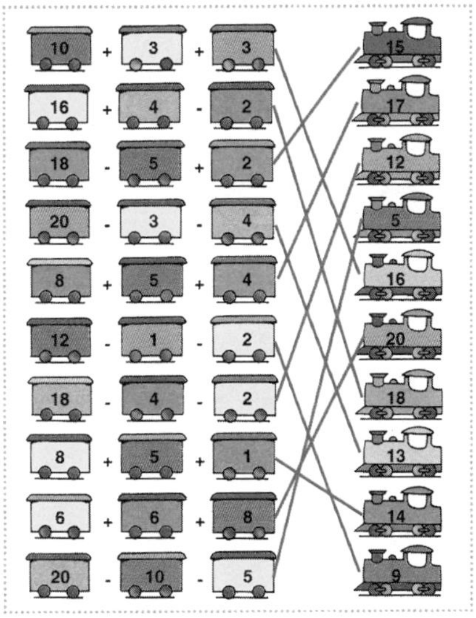
10 + 3 + 3
16 + 4 - 2
18 - 5 + 2
20 - 3 - 4
8 + 5 + 4
12 - 1 - 2
18 - 4 - 2
8 + 5 + 1
6 + 6 + 8
20 - 10 - 5
15
17
12
5
16
20
18
13
14
9

page 41

1. The horse is mad lad
2. On the lake I see a goat boat
3. Jack is sleeping late mate
4. The weather is mine fine
5. His hair is red mad
6. The mountain is fig big
7. I live in a beautiful house mouse
8. I would like to eat a peach beach
9. She is cooking meat meet
10. Mary is reading a book look

page 42

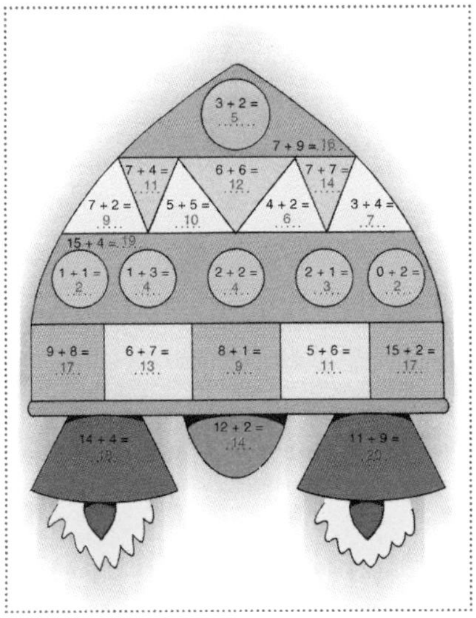
3 + 2 = 5
7 + 9 = 16
7 + 4 = 11
6 + 6 = 12
7 + 7 = 14
7 + 2 = 9
5 + 5 = 10
4 + 2 = 6
3 + 4 = 7
15 + 4 = 19
1 + 1 = 2
1 + 3 = 4
2 + 2 = 4
2 + 1 = 3
0 + 2 = 2
9 + 8 = 17
6 + 7 = 13
8 + 1 = 9
5 + 6 = 11
15 + 2 = 17
14 + 4 = 18
12 + 2 = 14
11 + 9 = 20

page 43

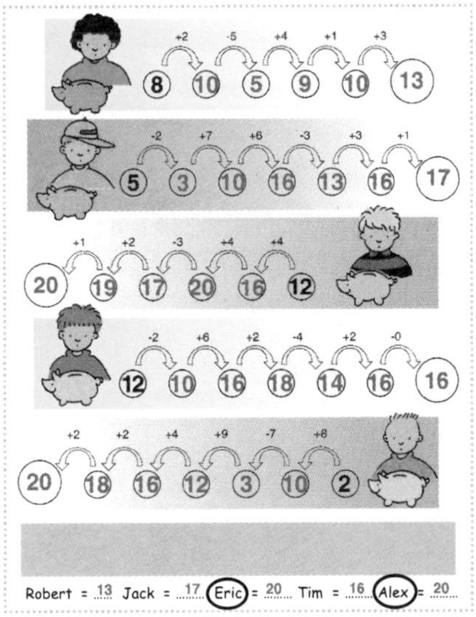
+2 -5 +4 +1 +3
8 10 5 9 10 13
-2 +7 +6 -3 +3 +1
5 3 10 16 13 16 17
+1 +2 -3 +4 +4
20 19 17 20 16 12
-2 +6 +2 -4 +2 -0
12 10 16 18 14 16 16
+2 +2 +4 +9 -7 +8
20 18 16 12 3 10 2
Robert = 13 Jack = 17 Eric = 20 Tim = 16 Alex = 20

page 44

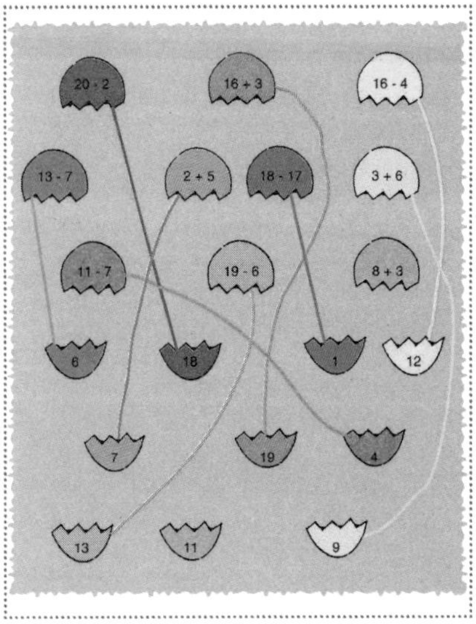
20 - 2
16 + 3
16 - 4
13 - 7
2 + 5
18 - 17
3 + 6
11 - 7
19 - 6
8 + 3
6
18
1
12
7
19
4
13
11
9

page 45

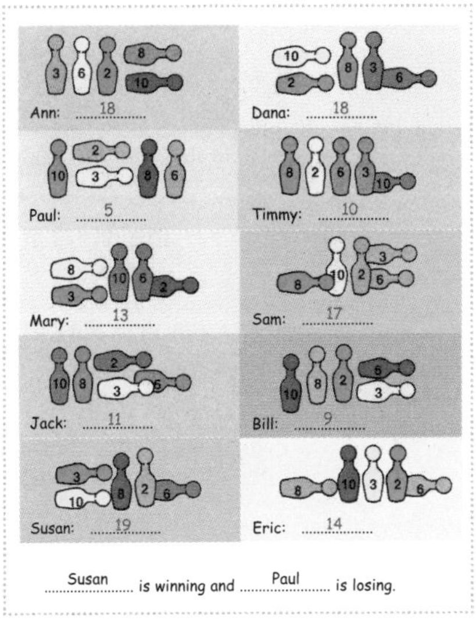
Ann: 18
Dana: 18
Paul: 5
Timmy: 10
Mary: 13
Sam: 17
Jack: 11
Bill: 9
Susan: 19
Eric: 14
Susan is winning and Paul is losing.

page 46

R = 14 S = 12 A = 10
H = 6 E = 11 D = 9
O = 18 B = 13 K = 15
Read
8 - 2 = 6 = H
19 - 8 = 11 = E
17 - 3 = 14 = R
8 + 3 = 11 = E
36 - 26 = 10 = A
16 - 7 = 9 = D
20 - 8 = 12 = S
20 - 10 = 10 = A
39 - 26 = 13 = B
36 - 18 = 18 = O
11 + 7 = 18 = O
12 + 3 = 15 = K
Write the sentence here.
He reads a book

page 47

The bird is on its nest.
The bird is in front of its nest.
The bird is in its nest.
Jack is on the fence.
Jack is at the left side of the fence.
Jack is in front of the fence.
Eric is at the farmer.
Eric is on the farmer.
Eric is in front of the farmer
The raven eats the cheese.
The fox eats the cheese.
The fox eats the raven.
The cow is on the pen.
The cow is in front of the pen.
The cow is in the pen.
The cloud comes in front of the Sun.
The Sun comes in front of the cloud.
The cloud comes near the Sun.

page 48

- 14 = 7 + 7
- 10 = 9 + 1
- 18 = 12 + 6
- 15 = 7 + 8
- 20 = 18 + 2
- 9 = 4 + 5
- 17 = 7 + 10
- 19 = 7 + 12
- 16 = 2 + 14

- 16 = 19 - 3
- 17 = 18 - 1
- 10 = 20 - 10
- 15 = 20 - 5
- 12 = 19 - 7
- 9 = 15 - 6
- 14 = 16 - 2
- 8 = 19 - 11
- 11 = 20 - 9

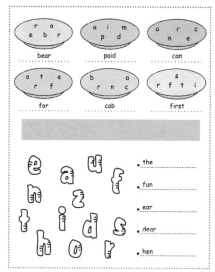

page 49

r a e b r — bear

a i m p d — paid

a r c n e — can

o t e r f — for

b a r n c — cab

s r f t i — first

- the
- fun
- ear
- dear
- hen

page 50

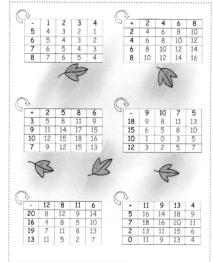

-	1	2	3	4
5	4	3	2	1
6	5	4	3	2
7	6	5	4	3
8	7	6	5	4

+	2	4	6	8
2	4	6	8	10
4	6	8	10	12
6	8	10	12	14
8	10	12	14	16

+	2	5	8	6
3	5	8	11	9
9	11	14	17	15
10	12	15	18	16
7	9	12	15	13

-	9	10	7	5
18	9	8	11	13
15	6	5	8	10
10	1	0	3	5
12	3	2	5	7

-	12	8	11	6
20	8	12	9	14
16	4	8	5	10
19	7	11	8	13
13	11	5	2	7

+	11	9	13	4
5	16	14	18	9
7	18	16	20	11
2	13	11	15	6
0	11	9	13	4

page 51

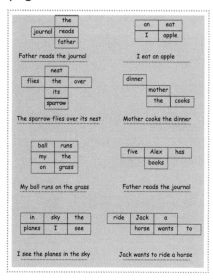

the / journal / reads / father

Father reads the journal

an / eat / I / apple

I eat an apple

nest / flies / the / over / its / sparrow

The sparrow flies over its nest

dinner / mother / the / cooks

Mother cooks the dinner

ball / runs / my / the / on / grass

My ball runs on the grass

five / Alex / has / books

Father reads the journal

in / sky / the / planes / I / see

I see the planes in the sky

ride / Jack / a / horse / wants / to

Jack wants to ride a horse

page 52

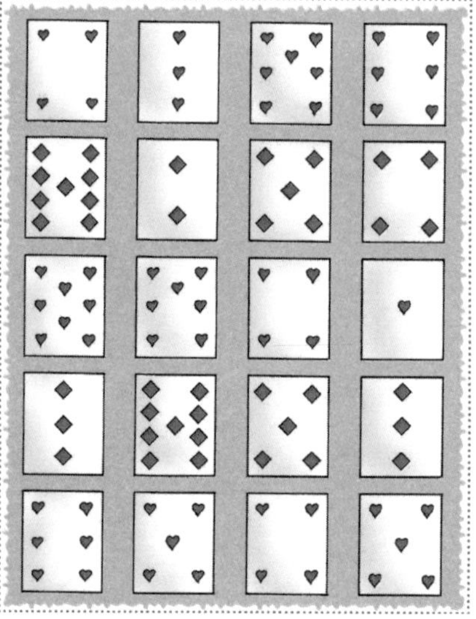

page 53

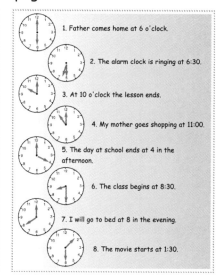

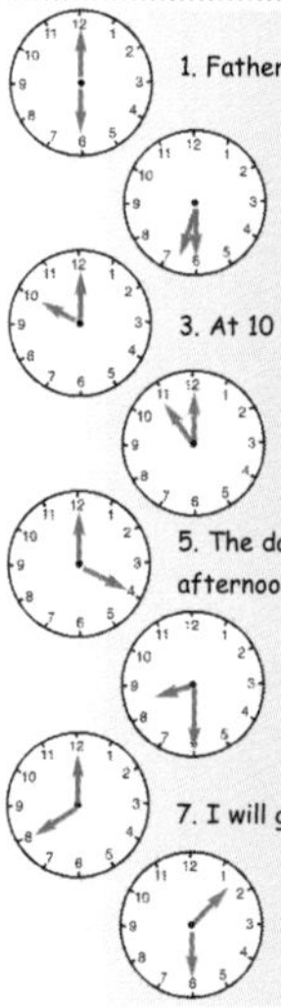

1. Father comes home at 6 o'clock.
2. The alarm clock is ringing at 6:30.
3. At 10 o'clock the lesson ends.
4. My mother goes shopping at 11:00.
5. The day at school ends at 4 in the afternoon.
6. The class begins at 8:30.
7. I will go to bed at 8 in the evening.
8. The movie starts at 1:30.

page 54

7 points
3 points
4 points
2 points
10 points
6 points
Jack: 9 points
Alex: 13 points
Eric: 16 points
Dan: 18 points
Timmy: 8 points
Bill: 17 points

page 55

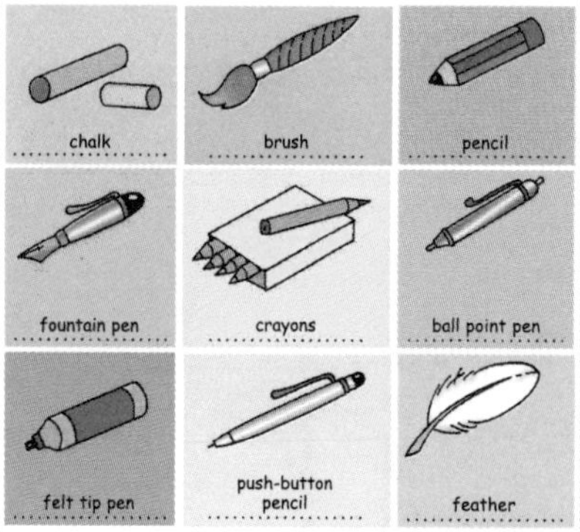
chalk
brush
pencil
fountain pen
crayons
ball point pen
felt tip pen
push-button pencil
feather

page 56

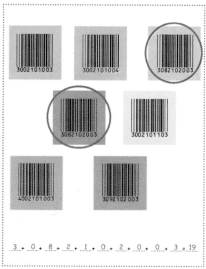

3002101003 — 3002101004 — 3082102003 — 3082102003 — 3002101103 — 4002101003 — 3092102003

3 + 0 + 8 + 2 + 1 + 0 + 2 + 0 + 0 + 3 = 19

page 57

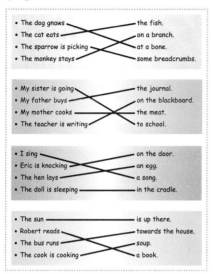

• The dog gnaws	the fish.
• The cat eats	on a branch.
• The sparrow is picking	at a bone.
• The monkey stays	some breadcrumbs.

• My sister is going	the journal.
• My father buys	on the blackboard.
• My mother cooks	the meat.
• The teacher is writing	to school.

• I sing	on the door.
• Eric is knocking	an egg.
• The hen lays	a song.
• The doll is sleeping	in the cradle.

• The sun	is up there.
• Robert reads	towards the house.
• The bus runs	soup.
• The cook is cooking	a book.

page 58

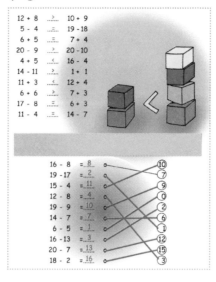

12 + 8	>	10 + 9
5 - 4	=	19 - 18
6 + 5	=	7 + 4
20 - 9	>	20 - 10
4 + 5	<	16 - 4
14 - 11	>	1 + 1
11 + 3	=	12 + 4
6 + 6	>	7 + 3
17 - 8	=	6 + 3
11 - 4	=	14 - 7

16 - 8 = 8	10
19 - 17 = 2	7
15 - 4 = 11	9
12 - 8 = 4	0
19 - 9 = 10	2
14 - 7 = 7	6
6 - 5 = 1	1
16 - 13 = 3	12
20 - 7 = 13	15
18 - 2 = 16	3

page 59

page 60

Stan
Becky
tree
Mark
Julie
Ann
Bob

page 61

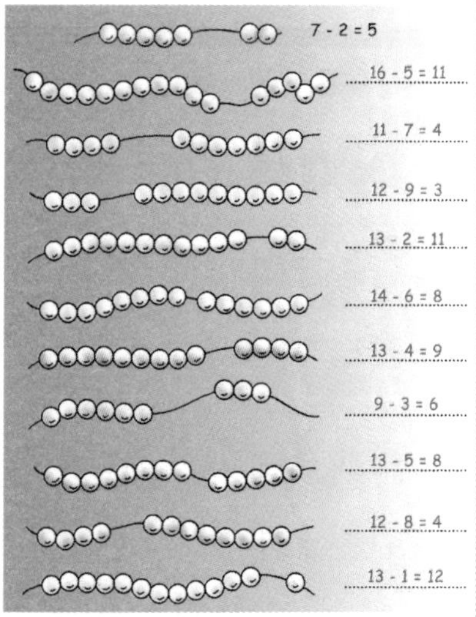
7 - 2 = 5
16 - 5 = 11
11 - 7 = 4
12 - 9 = 3
13 - 2 = 11
14 - 6 = 8
13 - 4 = 9
9 - 3 = 6
13 - 5 = 8
12 - 8 = 4
13 - 1 = 12

page 62

page 63

5 + 1 = 3 + 3
4 + 3 = 2 + 5
4 - 0 = 2 + 2
5 - 2 = 7 - 4
10 + 5 = 16 - 1

6 + 6 = 4 + 8
9 + 9 = 20 - 2
6 + 1 = 5 + 2
12 - 4 = 5 + 3
18 - 1 = 7 + 10

14 - 2 = 6 + 6
15 - 7 = 9 - 1
7 + 2 = 8 + 1
14 - 2 = 10 + 2
3 + 9 = 10 + 2

page 64

There is a dog cage on the left side of the house.
The house has a door.
There is smoke over the chimney.
The cat sleeps on the roof.
A cloud covers the sun.
There is a bicycle on the right side of the house.

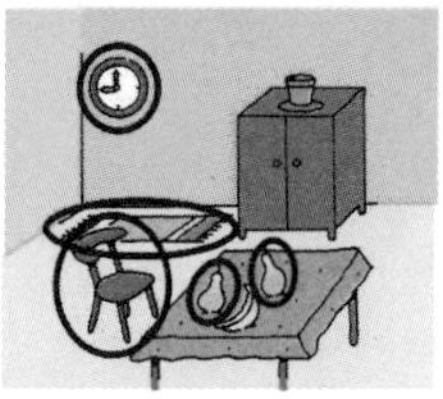

There is a pear on the table.
The closet is closed.
There is a vase on the closet.
It's two o'clock.
The chair is toppled over on the floor.
There is a carpet in front of the closet.

page 65

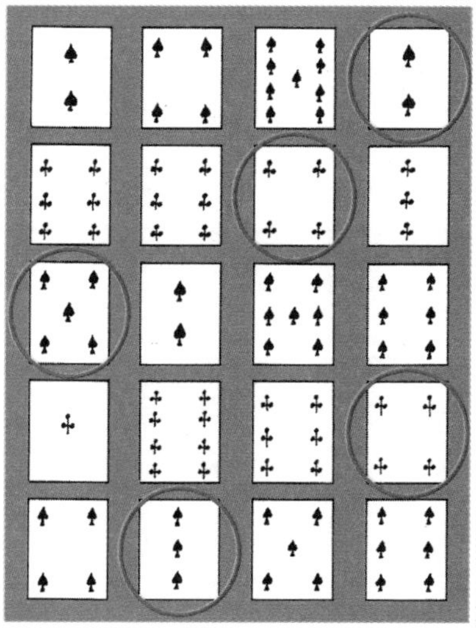

page 66

3 4 5 7 10
1 2 6 8 9

page 67

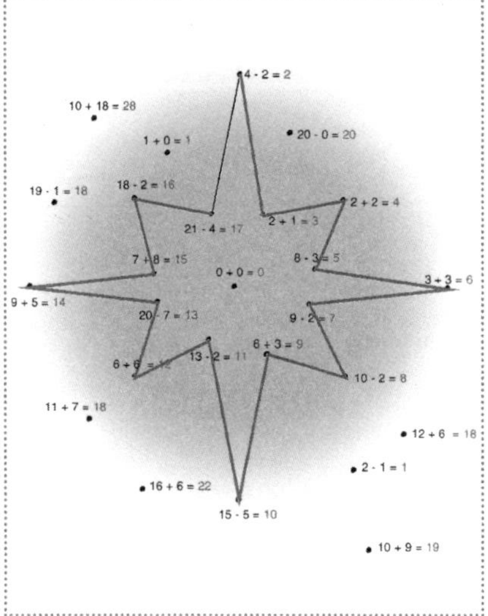
4 - 2 = 2
10 + 18 = 28
1 + 0 = 1
20 - 0 = 20
19 - 1 = 18
18 - 2 = 16
2 + 2 = 4
21 - 4 = 17
2 + 1 = 3
7 + 8 = 15
8 - 3 = 5
0 + 0 = 0
3 + 3 = 6
9 + 5 = 14
20 - 7 = 13
9 - 2 = 7
6 + 3 = 9
6 + 6 = 12
13 - 2 = 11
10 - 2 = 8
11 + 7 = 18
12 + 6 = 18
2 - 1 = 1
16 + 6 = 22
15 - 5 = 10
10 + 9 = 19

page 68

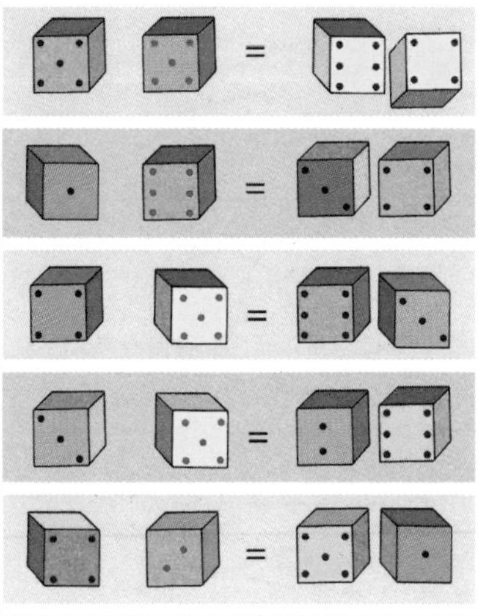

page 69

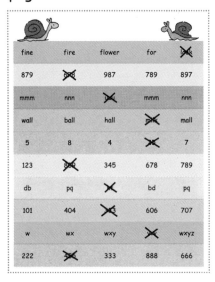

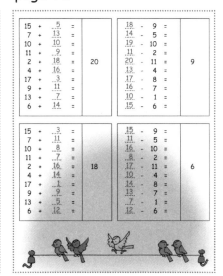

fine	fire	flower	for	~~look~~
879	~~678~~	987	789	897
mmm	nnn	X	mmm	nnn
wall	ball	hall	~~milk~~	mall
5	8	4	X	7
123	X	345	678	789
db	pq	X	bd	pq
101	404	X	606	707
w	wx	wxy	X	wxyz
222	~~456~~	333	888	666

page 70

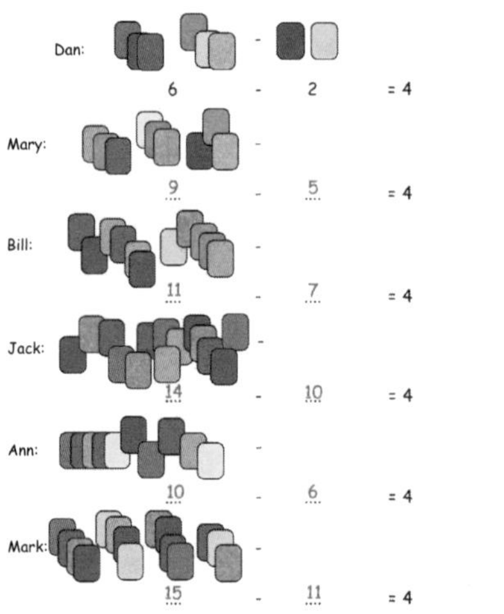
Dan: 6 - 2 = 4
Mary: 9 - 5 = 4
Bill: 11 - 7 = 4
Jack: 14 - 10 = 4
Ann: 10 - 6 = 4
Mark: 15 - 11 = 4

page 71

15	+	5	=	20	18	-	9	=	9
7	+	13	=		14	-	5	=	
10	+	10	=		19	-	10	=	
11	+	9	=		11	-	2	=	
2	+	18	=		20	-	11	=	
4	+	16	=		13	-	4	=	
17	+	3	=		17	-	8	=	
9	+	11	=		16	-	7	=	
13	+	7	=		10	-	1	=	
6	+	14	=		15	-	6	=	

15	+	3	=	18	15	-	9	=	6
7	+	11	=		11	-	5	=	
10	+	8	=		16	-	10	=	
11	+	7	=		8	-	2	=	
2	+	16	=		17	-	11	=	
4	+	14	=		10	-	4	=	
17	+	1	=		14	-	8	=	
9	+	9	=		13	-	7	=	
13	+	5	=		7	-	1	=	
6	+	12	=		12	-	6	=	

page 72

S
W
S
S
S
W
W
S
S

page 73

page 74

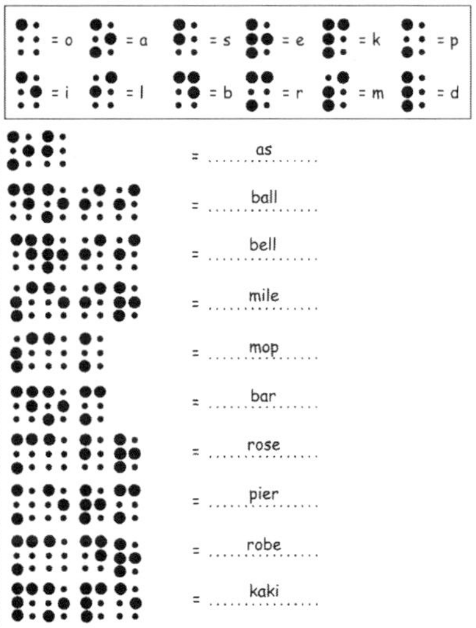
= o
= a
= s
= e
= k
= p
= i
= l
= b
= r
= m
= d
= as
= ball
= bell
= mile
= mop
= bar
= rose
= pier
= robe
= kaki

page 75

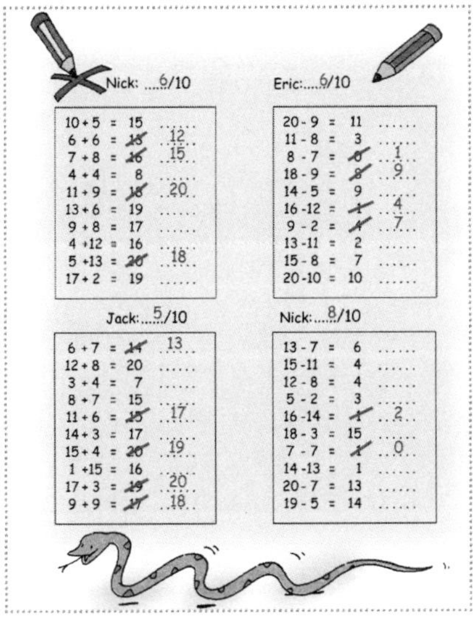
Nick: ...6/10
10 + 5 = 15
6 + 6 = 13 12
7 + 8 = 16 15
4 + 4 = 8
11 + 9 = 18 20
13 + 6 = 19
9 + 8 = 17
4 + 12 = 16
5 + 13 = 20 18
17 + 2 = 19
Eric: ...6/10
20 - 9 = 11
11 - 8 = 3
8 - 7 = 0 1
18 - 9 = 8 9
14 - 5 = 9
16 - 12 = 1 4
9 - 2 = 4 7
13 - 11 = 2
15 - 8 = 7
20 - 10 = 10
Jack: ...5/10
6 + 7 = 14 13
12 + 8 = 20
3 + 4 = 7
8 + 7 = 15
11 + 6 = 15 17
14 + 3 = 17
15 + 4 = 20 19
1 + 15 = 16
17 + 3 = 19 20
9 + 9 = 17 18
Nick: ...8/10
13 - 7 = 6
15 - 11 = 4
12 - 8 = 4
5 - 2 = 3
16 - 14 = 1 2
18 - 3 = 15
7 - 7 = 1 0
14 - 13 = 1
20 - 7 = 13
19 - 5 = 14

page 76

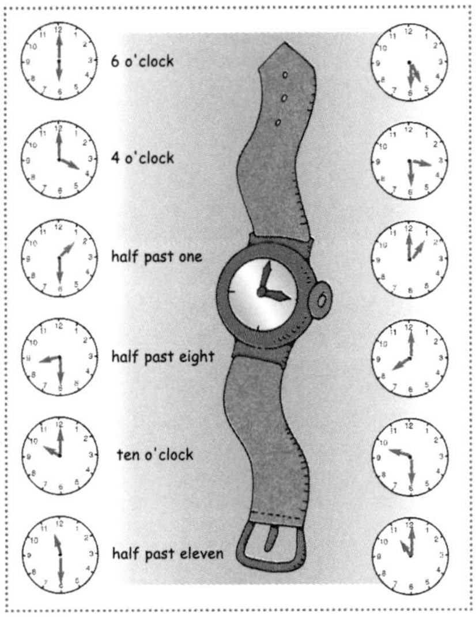
6 o'clock
4 o'clock
half past one
half past eight
ten o'clock
half past eleven

page 77

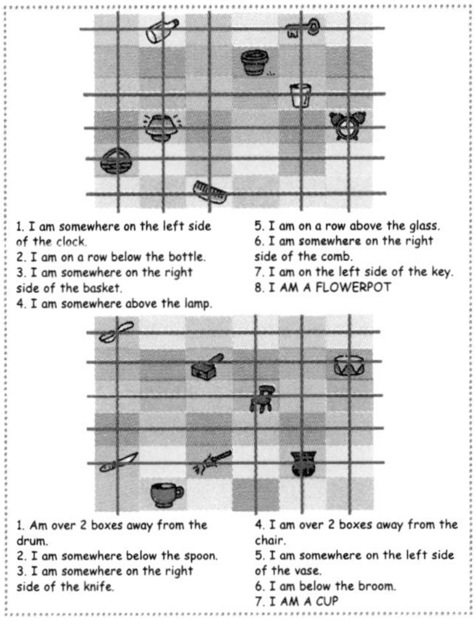
1. I am somewhere on the left side of the clock.
2. I am on a row below the bottle.
3. I am somewhere on the right side of the basket.
4. I am somewhere above the lamp.
5. I am on a row above the glass.
6. I am somewhere on the right side of the comb.
7. I am on the left side of the key.
8. I AM A FLOWERPOT
1. Am over 2 boxes away from the drum.
2. I am somewhere below the spoon.
3. I am somewhere on the right side of the knife.
4. I am over 2 boxes away from the chair.
5. I am somewhere on the left side of the vase.
6. I am below the broom.
7. I AM A CUP

page 78

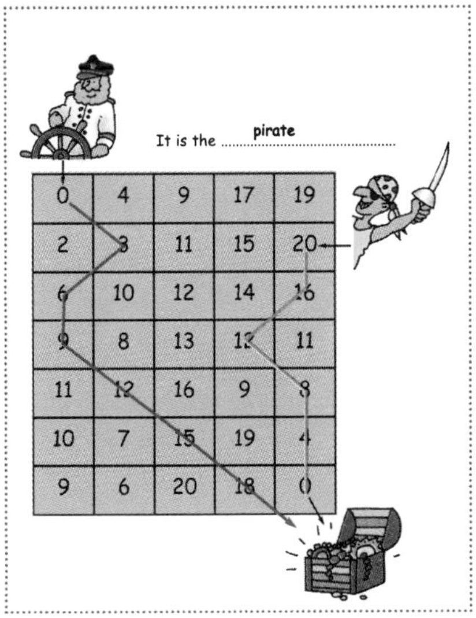
It is the pirate
0 4 9 17 19
2 3 11 15 20
6 10 12 14 16
9 8 13 12 11
11 12 16 9 8
10 7 15 19 4
9 6 20 18 0

page 79

20 +6 14 +5 9 +4 5 +3 2
19 -4 15 -3 12 -4 8 -3 5
19 +5 14 +4 10 +3 7 +2 5
17 -9 8 -2 6 -5 1 -1 0

page 80

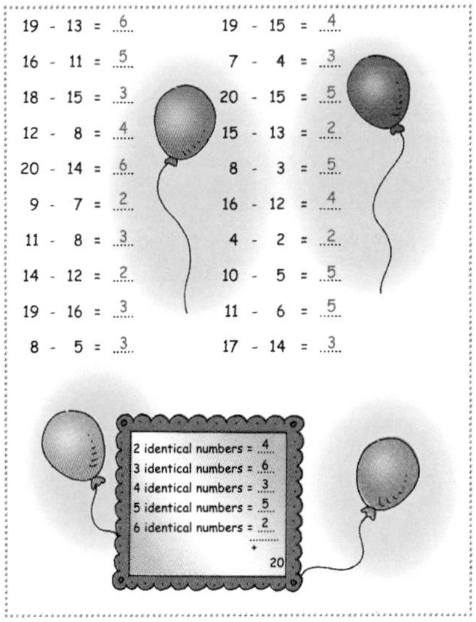
19 - 13 = 6
16 - 11 = 5
18 - 15 = 3
12 - 8 = 4
20 - 14 = 6
9 - 7 = 2
11 - 8 = 3
14 - 12 = 2
19 - 16 = 3
8 - 5 = 3
19 - 15 = 4
7 - 4 = 3
20 - 15 = 5
15 - 13 = 2
8 - 3 = 5
16 - 12 = 4
4 - 2 = 2
10 - 5 = 5
11 - 6 = 5
17 - 14 = 3
2 identical numbers = 4
3 identical numbers = 6
4 identical numbers = 3
5 identical numbers = 5
6 identical numbers = 2
+
20